Was it him?

It didn't look like Jon. It didn't look like anything human and alive. The flesh of the arms had
shrunk tight around the joints, around bones.
Blue veins protruded. The narrow length of the
body under the sheet was marked in stages,
curving ribs, jutting hip bones, toes at attention
at the ends of wasted legs. The visible bones of
the face stood out, practically in bas-relief. The
lips were slack, loose. It didn't look like Jon —
it didn't feel like Jon — but it was.

DAVID AND JONATHAN

CYNTHIA VOIGT

SCHOLASTIC INC.
New York Toronto London Auckland Sydney

ISBN 0-590-45166-9

12 11 10 9 8 7 6 5 4 3 2 1   5   4 5 6 7 8 9/9

Printed in the U.S.A.

To Robin

1967

He walked down the length of the room, between two rows of beds where the wounded lay, or sat — lines as straight and unvarying as the crosses in military cemeteries. He made his way around carts set out in the aisle, from which those who could eat were being served apples, peanut butter, crackers. Nobody questioned him; if they had he wouldn't have responded, perhaps because he hadn't heard. In December, a filmy tropical light filled the room, a heavy tropical heat weighted the air.

He went on, to the private cubicles at the end of the long room, the military version of Intensive Care. The man he was looking for lay in one of these. Alone, motionless, silent. The hospital sheet had been folded back to make a straight line over his chest. The emaciated arms rested

1

on top of the sheet, alongside the body. The top half of his head seemed swollen out with its wrapped bandages; glucose dripped steadily into his arm.

It didn't look like Jon. It didn't look like anything human and alive. The flesh of the arms had shrunk tight around joints, around bones. Blue veins protruded. The narrow length of the body under the sheet was marked in stages, curving ribs, jutting hip bones, toes at attention at the ends of wasted legs. The visible bones of the face stood out, practically in bas-relief. The lips were slack, loose. It didn't look like Jon — it didn't feel like Jon — but it was. Henry Marr, surgeon, Captain pro tem, USA, moved up to the head of the bed and put his hand on Jon's shoulder, wondering if now he was going to have to watch Jon die.

The round joint etched itself into his fingers. The man on the bed slept on, deeply sedated. After a long time, Henry moved to the foot of the bed and picked up Jon's chart.

The CO was in the canteen drinking out of a plastic cup, instant coffee thick with saccharine and Pream. "Marr. I put you on call for tonight."

Henry sat down opposite the Colonel, folded his arms on the Formica-topped table.

"You all right?"

"Yes," Henry said. "Tired."

"So what else is new. You should have been gone from here months ago. Don't get me wrong,

2

Marr, I appreciate your help and value your services — but you really ought to take one of those positions the hospitals stateside keep offering you. If I had any time free I'd worry about you, Marr."

"I can identify one of those men who came in last night, one of the prisoners."

"Spinal or head wounds?"

"Nafiche, Jonathan. He went missing in May. The head wounds."

"I'll get the records over. You're positive?"

"Yes."

The Colonel drank coffee, considered. "Have you seen the X-rays?"

Henry hadn't.

"Someone you know?"

"I grew up with him."

"You'll be first in line to do the work on him."

"You can't operate on him now — he'd never survive it."

"Take a look at the X-rays, see what you say then."

"I can't do it," Henry said. He was the best man at Special Surgical to do it.

The Colonel shrugged. "Maybe the question won't come up. It looks like some shell blew right beside him." '

"Can't he go to Tokyo? They're equipped — I know someone in Boston I can ask to fly over. We could send him to Tokyo."

"We could do that," the Colonel agreed, "but the chances are all he'd need at that end would

3

be a body bag. Splinters all over the place, Marr, and one's been driven in deep. Which may be moving, it probably is, and if he starts hemorrhaging the Army'll have another basket case to support for the rest of his life, if it doesn't finish him off. Take a look at the pictures," he advised.

Throughout the evening and all the next day, Henry waited for Jon to die or become conscious. When Jon didn't die, they immobilized him in the bed, setting his head between metal brackets to hold it still, running girths across chest, pelvis, wrists, ankles. When he could, when duties didn't keep him away, Henry sat in a stiff hospital chair by the side of Jon's bed.

The times he had seen Jon asleep. That first year at Harvard when he never knew — opening the door into their double — whether or not he'd find Jon sprawled asleep over some girl, any hour of the day, any hour of the night, and the room redolent of her perfume and sex, until finally he'd asked, "What is it, are you trying to plank every female in Cambridge?" Jon just grinned. "You jealous, Hank?" Henry hadn't answered. "Maybe you could hang a sign on the door to warn me?" Henry asked. "Warn? That's a curious word choice, don't you think? What should the sign say? Caution, children at play? *Mene mene tekel upharsim*? Or how about *caveat emptor*, although I am proud to say that *emptor* doesn't come into it at all. In case you're wondering." Jon was determined to misunderstand,

4

so Henry didn't argue. He moved into a single. Jon took up politics, and one particular girl. Henry took pre-med, and stood best man when Jon got married. Jon went to Chicago "to study languages, learning more ways to say exactly the same thing." Henry went to medical school. Usually, Henry waited for Jon to call him, Chicago to Boston, not wanting to intrude on a married man with his first child on the way; whatever he might have to ask Jon could usually wait. When he asked, Jon advised him to go into Obstetrics. "It's surgery I've got the natural ability for," Henry argued, "and half the time, with surgery, all you can do is . . . prolong things, or limit the damage." "That's too bad." Jon's voice mocked him. "C'mon, Jon, you know what I mean. What do you think?" "I'd do Obstetrics, if it were me." "But you — you always make things different. You like to jolly things up." "You're underestimating me, Hank. You shouldn't do that, you of all people." Henry didn't say anything. "Besides," Jon had asked, "what about the other half of the time?"

Remembering, Henry drank mug after mug of tea, watching Jon not die, and remembered. Worlds away to the west, on that arm of land thrusting out into the Atlantic, it would be cold, bitter December cold. There, the falling tides would leave lacy strands of ice along pale beaches, like offerings to the solid land. Here, it might as well be April, April dressed out in the colors and textures of August, deep spiky

5

greens, a violence of velvety pink-and-orange bloom. Henry didn't know which most dislocated him, the failure of seasons or the absence of ocean. Ocean, he thought, to bring the eternal note of sadness in: As it is written. Certainly the eternal note of something, the long tolling sound of a breaker unrolling itself up along the sands.

And this didn't even look like Jon. Jon looked — he looked like a bridegroom, life's bridegroom or something — the way he looked at his wedding where Henry had watched Jon watching Laurie, dark eyes alight with love and longing and laughter. But they drafted him, right after he got his doctorate — and he'd reenlisted. *That* he hadn't called Henry to announce. Henry couldn't imagine what time and this patch of history might have done to Jon, so that when the body on the bed at last stirred, Henry leaned forward, ready to know anything and to accept it.

When he put his hand on Jon's starved shoulder, he felt the tremor even there.

"So — Mor-iar-ty," Jon's voice croaked. "We — meet — again."

"I *was* hoping not to see you." The absolute truth.

"Hank. I," the mouth moved stiffly "just — woke up. You can't — be angry at me — already."

"No, I can't," Henry agreed.

"Henry," Jon said. "Henry." He lay quiet,

breathing. "I'm strapped — down."

"We don't want you to move. How do you feel? I know it's a stupid question."

"I feel — strapped down. Terrible."

"Hungry?"

"No." He waited, then spoke again. "This — Special Surgical?"

"Yes. We're going to need you to eat."

"Tired."

"I'm not surprised. It's OK. Go back to sleep."

"In — a minute." Jon waited, as if he had strength he could gather. "You were — going home. In July." He gave Henry time to answer. "I hurt," he said. "Henry?"

"I'll give you a shot."

"I can't — see."

"Bandages," Henry explained, standing up.

"That all?"

"No." He waited. Jon waited. "Do you want to hear about it now?"

"You — in charge?"

"I guess so."

"Then — tell me — in the morning. As it is written — sufficient — unto the day — is the good news," a breath, "thereof."

Henry turned around, to look at the figure on the bed. "That's not the way it's written at all."

"My shot," Jon reminded him.

For the season, the wards were decorated with aluminum Christmas trees, with plastic wreaths, with cards hung on strings along the walls. On one of his stops to look in on Jon, Henry removed a wreath from the curtains that isolated him. A nurse looked up at him, without the nerve to ask. "He's Jewish," Henry explained. "It doesn't say," the nurse answered. Henry picked up the chart from the end of the bed and marked in, Jewish.

"You're not eating enough," he said to the immobilized figure.

"What's *happened* to you, Hank? You didn't used to be such a grouch."

Henry didn't bother answering. He pulled a chair up close to Jon's head and sat down. "How do you feel?"

"Better. You can't imagine how much better. Terrible. How do I look?"

Henry didn't know what to say.

"That bad?"

"Yes. I've got some broth, clear, probably chicken, probably instant, and you're not going to like it much. Open your mouth."

After a while Jon's mouth opened. Henry trickled a spoonful of liquid into it. He watched the throat move. "Anyway, you sound better. Open."

Jon took a second spoonful.

"We need to feed you up," Henry said.

"Yeah, the last time I took a good look at myself I didn't look too good."

"You aren't cooperating. Open."

"I'm too tired."

"Jon — " Henry wasn't surprised. Every vineyard, he thought with a kind of satisfaction, could be made barren, given world enough and time. He went through the motions, insisting. "Jon."

"I'm OK tired, Henry. It's not what you think."

"How do you know what I think?"

"I do, I just do. Can we argue about it later?"

There was no question, there was no choice; he would have to go through with it by going through with it. Henry fed Jon eggnog and beef broth.

"I could eat better if you'd let me sit up," Jon said. "This eggnog could use some brandy."

"Somebody's going to have to operate."

"You?"

Henry didn't answer.

"You know what the Talmud says."

No, Henry didn't and Jon knew that perfectly well.

"The best of physicians is destined for Gehenna. How *do* I look?"

The image that came immediately to Henry's mind was a photograph of the survivors against the wire fences of the death camps. "Did you ever see anyone with polio?" he asked.

"Just pictures," Jon said. "Who would have thought seven months of bad food could do so much damage. Did you ever think, Hank, that this is the seventh month? I got through the first six, kind of waiting for this one, figuring if I heard a big voice saying *It is good* I was going to have to do some serious thinking about my understanding of the universe."

Henry didn't believe that for a minute. He fed Jon soup and eggnog.

"They knew we were there. All along. They *knew*, and they didn't do anything."

"They couldn't have known. If they had — "

"*I* knew someone was there, I knew there was a camp, a transit station, back in March I knew. So they knew. QED, Henry."

"Then why didn't — "

"How should I know? It doesn't do any good to get angry. That's not what I meant."

"Nothing does any good. Do you want to tell me about it?"

"Do you want to hear?"

"Don't be stupid."

"I'm not," Jon promised him. "Foolish maybe, probably, but not stupid. No, what I meant was, it was like being surrounded by David, like living inside David. I'm almost grateful to him."

"I'm not," Henry said.

"Granted. Although, you have to admit, he only worked on the material that was there. I figure, David wrapped me up and delivered me into that camp."

"That was history, not David. Tell me what you're driving at."

"At the end — for three weeks, maybe more,

I lost track. Maybe it was less, maybe it was all one endless day, one unending night. Maybe it doesn't matter how long — in the end. At the end, they put me in a cage. Bamboo. Twelve bamboo sticks on each side, twelve at the top, twelve at the bottom, a perfect cube of twelve. Naked. They took my dog tags, wedding ring — just such a poor forked creature, Hank. All day, all night. Think about it."

Henry wasn't about to think about it. He swallowed, and swallowed again.

"If it hadn't been for David, I would never have gotten through. I was so ashamed. And frightened."

"What did you *do*?" Henry asked, before he had time to stop himself.

"Prayed. At least, I think I prayed — my memory's not too clear — it felt like prayer, Henry."

"No, I mean why did they do that? What did you do?"

"I was too critical of the food?"

That made no sense and Jon wasn't stupid. Henry pointed out the obvious. "Anyway, it's done now, it's over."

"It's behind me," Jon said. "But it's not done or finished for other people, is it? I have to keep reminding myself of that."

"Why?"

"Because — I'm so glad to have it over with I might forget. So I'd like to hear about you

11

getting married. Not getting married. Why haven't you?"

"What?"

"Tall, handsome, good professional status, wealthy. Terrific genes — "

"This is ridiculous, Jon."

"We're over thirty — "

"Barely — "

"Time to people the world with little Chapins."

"I don't see that that concerns you," Henry said.

"Do go all huffy and New Englandish on me, Hank."

"Grow up, Jon. Why don't you."

"I am, Henry. I have. What *are* you so frightened of?"

Henry could have laughed. Staring at Jon, strapped down on a hospital bed because what one political-military establishment hadn't done to him the other had, or was about to — the question was almost enough to make him laugh.

Jon persisted. "Didn't I stand quietly by while you've spent — what? — fifteen years, keeping your life at arm's length? Listen, a parable. The Parable of the Talents. Once there was a master who was going away on a long journey. He had three servants. He gave each servant talents, for the time he would be away. The first servant got one, the second five — "

"But that's a real one," Henry protested.

"Hank, *this* is real," Jon said. "So think about it. I'm real and you're real, and David — "

"David is dead and has nothing to do with it. Not anymore."

"Wrong again, Henry," Jon said.

ONE

A single wave unrolled itself up along the beach. Low sandy dunes lay in a line, their sparse grasses leaning inland. A pale sky floated overhead, brushed with filmy clouds.

From behind one dune, a dark head appeared, warily raised. Everything seemed quiet, so the boy worked himself along with elbows and knees, hitching his shoulders as if he carried on his back not only his weapon but also rounds of ammunition. Seeing no one, no danger, he waved an arm high, signaling troops forward before he himself crawled slantwise down the dune. His broad face glistened with sweat; sweat matted his curly hair.

Had he looked along to the southwest, the boy would have seen the exulting enemy, deploying his own platoon with silent gestures. The silence continued until — sensing his moment — the enemy rose up, gave a cry of war, pulled a grenade from his belt to remove the pin with practiced teeth and hurled it at the dark-haired boy, who fell amazed and unmoving onto the sand. The enemy ran forward, hands spraying machine-gun fire.

The body lay face down. Its shoulders twitched. Henry Marr put his foot on the broad back and prepared to deliver a final bayonet stroke. The body rolled over, and grabbed Henry's calf, and flung him face down into the sand. When Henry raised his head, spitting sand from his mouth, Jon was still laughing.

"You fall for it, every time."

"Not every time." Henry spat again.

Jon ignored the quibble. "It's the oldest trick of them all, the possum trick, and you always fall for it. You'll never hold hill forty-four thousand, seven hundred sixteen that way — or whatever pimple of the earth they're killing one another over this time. Orientals are crafty — the North Koreans not excepted — just like the Jews." Jon sat cross-legged in the sunlight, savoring Henry's chagrin.

Henry sat up. "The grenade couldn't have missed. Or the machine gun cover. If you weren't killed, you'd still have been too badly wounded to flip me."

"Nope." Jon's face, except for the brown eyes, grew solemn. "I was too low for the spray shot, and the grenade — it was like your fast ball,

Hank, a little wild — landed over there. Blew up Shaughnessy, may his soul rest easy, he had promised to become a first-class fighting man. It left me untouched. As you see."

"C'mon, Jon, it hit you. Square."

"Missed. Missed by a mile. Look — " He held out an empty hand. "Shaughnessy's helmet. He did the right thing, giving his life to save his commanding officer."

"That's ridiculous."

"Then would you believe," holding up the other empty hand, "Shaughnessy's boot? With the foot still in it?"

"That's revolting."

Jon dropped the offending object. He scrabbled in the sand in front of them. "Then what do you say to this? A photograph of Shaughnessy's sainted sister, pure as the driven snow, and it was to save her from the advances of little yellow men that he came killing to this innocent land. See? The glass isn't even cracked. Rest easy, oh, Bridget O'Brian O'Rourke, et cetera et cetera — your brother has gone to a better world than this, but I shall return, to claim your — "

Henry began to laugh helplessly, and Jon stopped speaking.

"Although," he started again, "Shaughnessy might not be rejoiced to have his sister folded in the embrace of a young lion of the Chosen People, lifting her moist lips and round arms — her et cetera et ceteras."

16

"You sound like you know what you're talking about."

"I always know what I'm talking about, I just don't often know what I'm saying. Think of Shaughnessy, though, he's a man with a problem. Should he allow his sister to marry me, and thereby ruin her life, even if I was his revered commanding officer — or should he lean down from whatever cloud he's harping on and bonk me with a shillelagh."

"By all means the shillelagh. That's two votes for the shillelagh," Henry called up to the sky.

"This is serious," Jon reminded him. "Wars have been fought for less, millions massacred on just this question."

They were silent then, looking over the distances of the bright sea, where a few boats marked the horizon.

"We're too old for these war games," Jon said at last.

"Fifteen's not too old."

"I'm sixteen and you're almost. We're almost old enough for the real thing. Although I don't think this Korean debacle will last long enough for you to get into it. Of course, there's always hope."

"If I had a sister, you could marry her," Henry said, and meant it.

"There speaks the last just man on Cape Cod." Jon stood up, dusting sand off his thick legs. Henry squinted up at him. "Although, since you don't have a sister, the problem remains academic. Also, if you did, she'd be some skinny, dried-up goy-girl, a stick like you. Besides, I'm too young to be thinking of marriage. Besides, look at the tide. Is it too cold for a dip? It has to be, I think it is. So, we should make our ritual baths today."

"It's only April, Jon — the cruelest month, remember? We have it on good authority, breeding lilacs out of the dead land."

"You don't believe that, do you, Hank? No, seriously, do you?"

Henry didn't answer. If Jon — who knew him so well — said he didn't, he probably didn't. If Jon thought he shouldn't, then he wouldn't, even if it was Jon who had introduced him to Eliot.

"Well?" Jon asked.

Henry shrugged. He thought he knew what Eliot meant, and he thought it was true. "I'm thinking."

Jon relented. "That's good enough for me." He reached out a hand to haul Henry up onto his feet.

"But the water's freezing," Henry protested.

Jon ignored him.

Henry ignored himself.

At the water's edge they stripped down to shorts. Bitter cold spray bit at their ankles and bare legs. Icy cold water ran up over their toes and feet.

"You're crazy," Henry told Jon. "You know that."

"In this world, there's nothing better than to

18

be crazy. The Parable of the Good Man Fallen into a Nest of Vipers."

Henry waited, mild sunlight warm as a cloak on his naked shoulders and back.

"I can't think of it. But he must have died miserably, don't you think? Now, you know the rules: in at least up to your shoulders, no shoving, no ducking of one another — it's free will here — entirely wet, head to toe. Ready?"

Henry hesitated.

"If you scream it doesn't feel nearly so cold," Jon promised him. "And for the love of Pete close your eyes, or your eyeballs will freeze in their sockets and I'll have to lead you home like Oedipus out of Thebes and what your mother will say to me — " Jon charged into the gray water, howling aloud, splashing wildly with his hands, finally diving headfirst into an oncoming wave.

Henry could have done the same, but he walked slowly into the water, to tolerate each increase of unbearable cold without flinching. Ankles, knees, thighs burned numb, loins, belly — his diaphragm heaved and tried to urge haste on him. He did not let himself hesitate, he did not let himself hurry. At the final step, when he stood in water up to his chin, he took a deep, painful breath, closed his eyes, and dipped. The icy wetness surrounded him. The cold dug into his bones. He had to concentrate to find the muscles in his thighs that would enable him to lift his head up, out of the water.

Objective accomplished, Henry turned back to the beach, shoving water aside with his chest and legs, until he splashed up onto the sand. They shook themselves like dogs, spraying water about, and Jon threw his arms up wide toward the sky. "Master of the Universe — we praise you for this day and these deep waters. OK, Hank, jumping jacks, a hundred."

Dry again, they lay side by side, eyes closed against the midday sun, in a companionable and mindless silence. An offshore breeze carried with it the whisper of pine branches behind them and the faint echo of rustling beach grass. When Henry opened his eyes to slits he could see the grainy pale sand beyond his toes, and the way the waves spread patches of damp, each edged with sea foam. When he closed his eyes again, he could hear the soft watery sound with which the waves greeted the wind.

Jon couldn't tolerate silence for long. "So," he asked, "what did your mother say about the job?"

Henry shrugged.

"Did you tell her?"

"Not yet."

"What do you think she'll say?"

"Good for you and where do I sign."

"She won't be upset about her little boy scouring nasty old pots and pans — "

"We need the money, we're always short of money."

" — and working for the only Jew in town — "

"That's not fair, Jon. You know she likes you."

"One of the sacred . . . I can never remember what it is . . . Chopins, Charlatans, Chopsticks — "

"Chapins. C'mon, Jon, you know that."

" — who graced the sacred floorboards of the sacred Mayflower with their sacred toenail clippings — "

"Lay off. Talk about people who are prejudiced — "

"Destined for Harvard, my dears — "

"I'm destined for any place that will give me a scholarship," Henry said.

Jon sat up, abruptly. "Unless your father could write a hit symphony. Imagine that, Hank. It's what I'd want if I were him, people humming my music in all twelves tones."

Henry grinned without bothering to open his eyes.

"It should be possible," Jon insisted. "When I think of the way a man like your father — you don't do him justice, Henry, he may just be a genius, how would *we* know about that. Enid says he is."

"It doesn't help *me* any."

"And the way he lives, the way you all live — "

"It's not Pig Alley."

"I'm sorry, Hank, I didn't mean it the way it sounded. It just burns me up, it really does. You know what I meant. I didn't mean — In a properly run world, a man like your father would be supported by the state, encouraged, and admired. You'd be at the top of the heap."

"In the properly run world you're thinking of," Henry raised himself onto his elbows to correct Jon, "my father would probably be dead — shot for refusing to join the Army, serve his country. Instead, he was put in jail."

"Not jail. A detention camp for CO's. That's different."

"Not for my mother it wasn't."

"Yeah, but she had her family to contend with. Especially after your uncle was shot down, they must have . . . I don't know, Hank, your grandmother sounds bad enough now. Imagine her in her full vigor."

Jon's face, except for the eyes, was entirely earnest, and if Henry hadn't known him so well for so long — ever since the first day of fifth grade nearly six years ago, when Henry stood up before the class of strangers to announce that his name was Henry Chapin Marr and he lived out on Beach Road and he came from Brooklyn and his father was a composer; and heard the snickers and saw the sideling looks between the kids, except for one bright-faced boy sitting in the back row who grinned as if this was all part of some huge joke he'd tell Henry about later — if it weren't Jon, Henry would have thought he meant only and exactly what he was saying.

"Did Enid really say that my father's a genius?"

"Would I lie to you? She knows what she's talking about, too," Jon added, "even if she is my sister. Enid knows music."

"Half sister," Henry corrected. "You know," he said, the sun warm on his belly, his eyes closed, "You and Enid have had pretty much exactly the same life. She was only five or six, wasn't she? when your parents had you?"

"Something like that."

"Then what's her gripe?"

"How should I know?" Jon answered. "Maybe — you know what they say, you give people half a glass of water and some will say it's half full and some will say it's half empty. She's a half-empty person. Me, I'm the half-full type, don't you think?"

Henry agreed. He pictured the glass. "But it's just half a glass of water."

Jon laughed. "There it is, the blazing blade of the actual, before which similes quake and allegories tremble, which cuts through analogy as through a Gordian knot."

"OK, OK. I take your meaning." Henry sat up, sheepish. "You think I have no imagination."

"I never said that. Did you ever hear me say that? I don't think I've thought it either. I think maybe *you* don't think you do; if you want to know what I think."

"And maybe I'm right," Henry maintained. "Does Enid?"

"Maybe that's what her difficulty is — " Jon

turned to face Henry, his face alight with the idea. "No, listen. Because she's always imagining about what she doesn't have. It's like when she was accepted at the Conservatory. She didn't talk about how hard it was to get into the Conservatory — and it is, believe me it is — she just talked about how much harder it is to get into other places, by implication better places, where she hadn't gotten in."

"I thought Enid just wanted to study music."

"She always feels — as if she's gotten the short end. You know, Why did I have to be born a girl, and why can't I sing C over high C. Never mind that she comes in true on the B-flat just under. Why did I have to be in Germany — "

"But she was only a baby."

"It was her father the Nazis executed."

"And she got out."

"She was actually there, along with people who didn't get out."

"But that doesn't make sense."

"I'm not saying I can figure her out. Maybe what she needs is a boyfriend."

"No she doesn't." The words were out of his mouth before Henry thought to stop them. Jon stared, speculating; his mouth opened. Henry spoke quickly, "She'd drive any guy crazy. Can you imagine being married to her?"

But Jon had seen through him. "Hank. Are we having a little case of primal lust?"

It wouldn't do any good to deny it; and there was no need. It was Jon who had asked Henry the liberating question — in the eighth grade, he thought, if he remembered correctly it was the eighth — "Do you know the great thing about masturbation, Hank? The great thing is, nobody gets pregnant." So Henry considered his emotions under the heading of primal lust — not love, which he had been afraid might be their right name, but lust, which made sense, and made everything all right. Lust was ordinary, lust was the right response to the swell of bosom and the mound of belly, and thighs, ass, neck, ear whorls — you couldn't do anything about lust, about feeling it. Henry didn't mind lusting after Enid; it was the possibility of loving her that had troubled him.

"And how long as this been going on?" Jon reached over to take Henry's pulse, timing it against an imaginary pocketwatch. "And why didn't I even suspect?"

Henry had no idea.

"Lust," Jon said, "is the thing with feathers that perches — "

"Lust is the expense of spirit in a waste of shame. Let's drop the subject."

"It's OK, I can understand it, really I can. She's got a terrific figure, and just because she isn't interested in anything except music, including you, and me, and everyone else, and just because she doesn't have any sense of humor — and there's the chosen race for you, Hank, if you're looking. Never mind who laughs last; who laughs at all, he who laughs, go for that. But I can really see why, Hank, why Enid, I don't blame you a bit. Until she opens her mouth."

"Enid's got a good voice," Henry maintained stoutly, stuffily. His laughter, bubbling up, betrayed him.

"Besides," Jon said, "you've got too much good sense to take it seriously."

That, Henry wasn't so sure of. But he'd have liked Jon to be right, so he answered, "Yeah. Sure. I mean, I don't like her. I don't *dis*like her, not that much, that's not it. It's what you said, lust. Just a little lust."

"Enid's OK if you don't let her get you down. The way she keeps insisting that the glass is half empty, her glass. And she doesn't remember drinking it."

"Maybe she thinks it spilled. When somebody else was holding it."

"Not bad, not bad at all. But, Hank, do you then toss the rest of the glass away?"

"Not if you're thirsty," Henry agreed.

"Or maybe especially if you're thirsty you do," Jon said thoughtfully.

The waves washed up on the sand, marking a receding tide. Sea gulls quarreled overhead. Thoughts of empty glasses and paradoxes and lust drifted through Henry's mind, wispy as clouds. Jon's voice interrupted him. "It's time for me — you coming?"

Henry always did. On Sundays, Jon walked or rode to Henry's house, Sunday mornings, because Henry and Jon spent Sundays together, doing whatever. If Jon had to work at the restaurant in the afternoon, Henry went along. Because Saturday was the Sabbath, Jon wasn't available, but Sundays they spent together. Henry stood up, brushed sand off his backside and elbows, and stretched lazily.

"On your mark," Jon said.

Henry didn't wait for the rest of the countdown. He raced up the dune, and Jon — who wasn't planning to wait either — started beside him. They crested the top of a dune with Henry slightly in the lead, and bounded down. On the down slope, Jon's longer, more muscular legs enabled him to pull ahead. Henry ran with shorter strides, at first to stay even, then to catch up, nearly leaping down the sandy slope. When his right leg crumpled beneath him he careened over, rolling on his shoulder, and slid until the sand stopped him, cursing under his breath, almost whispering.

His ears rang. Chills ran along the surface of his scalp. He put his hands over his eyes while waves of nausea washed over him, outwaiting them. "Shit," he whispered, "shit goddamit, oh, shit."

"Henry?"

He looked up at Jon's face and rolled his shoulders until he was squarely on his back. Shameful memory of the first time this had happened to him — how he had behaved — kept him mute.

27

Jon crouched down. "Your knee?"

"Damned kneecap."

"You ought to use words more carefully, Hank," Jon advised.

Shock faded, and Henry could think again, and trust himself to speak without hysterics. "I don't know what we're going to do. On this leg — once it's out of joint, it stays out." Distended muscles pulled down the side of his right thigh. He sensed — he knew he shouldn't look at his leg — the hollowness where his kneecap ordinarily gave a rounded shape. His stomach threatened again, to heave, and he clamped his mind down, hard, over the messages nerves were sending to his brain. You had to acknowledge the immutable, recognize it, and not waste your strength fighting it. Immutable right then was wrenched cartilage and stiffening tendons, the dislocated cap of his knee. "Goddammit," Henry said. He held his stomach tight.

"It has to be straightened out, right?" Jon studied Henry's bent leg. "It looks awful. Does it hurt?"

Henry shook his head. "Not much, yet. It mostly feels — wrong. Later is when it's painful." He closed his eyes and clenched his hands into fists. "You better get my mother. The doctor has to give the leg a shot — to relax the muscles — they stiffen up and that holds the kneecap out." Jon put a hand on Henry's thigh. "Jon? What are you waiting for? Get my mother, you heard me." The necessity of endurance could

28

break Henry, experience had taught him that, and he wanted help, help on the way, he wanted to know that; and he wanted to be alone when his spirit panicked, and deserted him.

"If we can get it right back in — that's what you're supposed to do. I've been looking into medical careers, reading first-aid books. But how come it's staying out? I thought it slid back into place by itself."

"That's the left leg, the left's the one that just — twists in place, sort of. It doesn't stay out. Don't mess around with it, OK? Please, Jon, just go tell my mother." Henry heard himself losing control, and clamped his lips shut.

Jon talked on. "I can't possibly carry you. I mean, I know I'm more physically mature and in good shape, but even so you'd give me a hernia. Or seven. I don't know if I can actually do this, but your muscles'll be petrified in place if you wait here long enough for me to get your mother and then her to get the doctor. I should try, Hank."

He sounded apologetic, but when Henry briefly opened his eyes, Jon's eyes seemed to be laughing, pleased.

"First," Jon announced, "a brief anatomical review." He began to sing, his voice a reedy tenor. "De toe bone connected to de foot bone — Is that right? Sing along, Henry, the knee you save may be your own. De foot bone connected to de ankle bone, de ankle bone — "

Henry joined in; he needed to make noise,

29

any noise, even his off-key singing was better than loosing the whimpers that were crawling up inside his chest. As they sang, Jon's other hand closed firmly around Henry's right calf, just above the ankle. "De knee bone connected to — "

Henry had an impulse to giggle that was not much different from his impulse to whimper. His whole body was tense, to endure until Jon finally admitted that he was going to have to ride his bike to Henry's house. Jon's voice bellowed away, "Hip bone connected — " and Henry bellowed with him. At the same time, Jon pulled firmly on Henry's ankle, simultaneously forcing the thigh steadily down.

Henry stopped singing. "Don't," he said. "Please don't, Jon," he said. The kneecap slid back into its socket with a muted, snapping sound.

After a few minutes, Henry heard Jon's voice, wavering. "Am I going to be sick?"

"Not on me, please. Did you do it? I don't want to look."

"Doesn't it feel healed?"

"No. It feels offended."

Jon took off his damp T-shirt, and tied it around the knee. "It's not an Ace bandage, but — just so that it shouldn't slip out again on us. Here, up — " he hauled up on Henry's hand, until he could brace Henry's weight on his shoulder, "try standing, gently please, I'm not sure I could do that again — " And Henry stood, weight on his left leg, the right balancing delicately. "So, Hank, you think I could be a doctor?"

Henry nodded.

"Can you walk to the bikes, if I help?"

Henry nodded. His knee felt composed of jelly, but he made it the quarter mile to where they had leaned their bikes up against a scrubby pine. In the shade the air was cool. "Maybe you better get my mother to come pick me up," he said, looking at his bike and bracing his shoulder against a spiny trunk. "I guess that's it for the baseball team, do you think?"

"How long does this cripple you up for?" Jon asked.

"I can't remember. It hasn't happened to this leg for years, don't you remember? It was seventh grade last time, I walked with a cane and you carried my books."

"I remember you had a *lot* of books, more than anyone else. Why *did* you have so many books, Hank? I always meant to ask."

"Get my mother to bring the car. I'll wait here. I think it took a week, maybe two, to heal. Maybe he'll still give me a chance."

"Could you walk beside your bike, using it like a crutch?"

"The worst pain was the first night, I remember that. But maybe this time — you got it back in so fast maybe there won't be so much bruising. How did you know how to do that, Jon?"

"I told you, I've been reading up on first aid.

31

Dislocations are actually pretty simple. I mean, it's not like setting a bone, you can't really screw things up, the body won't let you. Or, if you wanted to just sit on your bike, I could wheel it along, and manage mine with the other hand maybe. The thing is, I have to get to work."

"Are you really thinking about medical school?" Henry asked.

"Just get up on the seat — if you brace the leg — "

Grateful for the orders, Henry obeyed. Jon steadied Henry's bike, then reached over to take his own by the handlebars. "Can you manage both?" Henry asked.

"We'll find out, won't we?"

Cautiously, Jon pushed. Henry had one hand on the handlebars and the other around his bandaged knee; his left leg he stuck out, to minimize the wobbling. Jon pushed on.

"So, do you want to hear about my career plan? Or not."

Henry really wanted to be left alone with his bad luck. "Sure," he said.

"They've been after me about a career," Jon began, his breath uneven with the strain of keeping all the machines and dependent bodies on an even keel. "Ever since my bar mitzvah. Now that I'm a man. It's been a long three years, I can tell you. But I think — I've figured out the way to handle it. What I think is — if I look into professions a few months at a time, that'll keep them distracted. You know? They can tell everybody, 'Our Jonathan? He wants to be a doctor, such an ambitious boy.' It can't do any harm and you find out some useful things. How to deal with dislocations, for example."

"Yeah. Thank you, Jon. I mean — thanks."

"I hope the list of possibilities will hold out until I get to college. Doctor, lawyer, Indian chief, dentist, accountant, veterinarian, cat burglar, the only one I can never mention is rabbinical school."

"Why not?" Henry asked, interested despite himself.

"The Rabbi would institute such a course of study — I'd never see daylight again. Such things are not accomplished easily, or quickly. I know some Hebrew, but for real study — take my word for it. Besides, it would break his heart, because I don't mean it."

Henry gritted his teeth against a streak of pain that burned up his leg. He pressed his hand more firmly against the knee. "So you don't want to be a doctor."

"I don't want to be anything, I just want my parents to be happy," Jon laughed. "I don't have your New England drive for achievement. Your stoic nature."

"You can't be a good soldier if you're afraid of pain — or confused by — doubts. Fears. Not an officer, anyway."

"Just think, Hank, when you're on the cover of *Time*, you and your five stars, I can say I knew you when. I can say, 'I knew him when he was just a squirt of a stoic.' Did I ever tell you that the Romans knew how to strangle themselves? Self-strangulation. Picture it, Hank. We should try it some time."

Henry smiled to himself. "I bet I could. If I wanted to."

"I bet you could," Jon agreed. "If you do, can I watch?"

"I don't know," Henry said, sputtering with laughter, "you didn't invite me to your bar mitzvah."

They rounded a corner precariously, Jon grunting. The road straightened, then curved again. "You know what I don't understand?" Jon asked.

Henry couldn't imagine.

"War," Jon said. "And God. War and God."

"Do you expect yourself to be able to understand that?"

Sometimes Henry could make Jon laugh, without even trying, as now, laughter that was almost celebration. "I know, I know. But — "

"You mean because every side thinks God is on theirs?"

"No — I wonder if we aren't still just fighting our way out of the garden."

"Garden? What garden?"

"Hank, you're a cultural wasteland."

"Oh. You mean Eden. But we got thrown out of that."

"That's *our* side of the story. Did you ever wonder what God's side is?"

"You're the one who thinks about God." Was Jon serious? He might be; he didn't have to be. "But what does that have to do with war?" he asked. "Even you can't look on war as a blessing, Jon, so don't try that on me."

"I wasn't going to. No, I don't. I just wonder . . ."

Henry waited. Then he asked, "You mean life as a testing place?"

"That would be such a waste, though, wouldn't it? Of the place and the creature. No, I wonder why you want to go into the military, for example," Jon said. "Who you're trying to prove what to."

"It's not that simple," Henry protested.

"I didn't say that was simple."

"You always have to have the last word," Henry complained.

Jon waited a long time, walking steadily along the sun-dappled road before he answered, "Of course, if you don't survive I guess things *are* simple."

TWO

Henry's mother had inherited their house —
one of the summer cottages on the beach road —
from a great-aunt five years earlier. By tradition,
it should have gone to one of the Chapin men,
but the only male Chapin of his mother's gen-
eration was her brother, William, killed in the
war. The house was too big for the three of them,
Henry supposed; it was too bad Uncle William
didn't survive to keep the property in the Chapin
name, he knew; but after their one-bedroom,
two-window apartment in Brooklyn Heights, he
couldn't be sorry to be living in the sprawling
clapboard house.

Two narrow tracks through the close-growing
scrub pines were all they had for a driveway,
long enough so the house couldn't be seen from
the road. Jon dropped his bike by the roadside

and wheeled Henry along, missing most of the potholes. Henry collapsed on the steps to the back door. Jon went inside, to find an Ace bandage and Henry's mother.

If Henry opened his eyes, he would see piney woods. If he opened his eyes, leaned around and turned his head, he would see young green grass, and the sea beyond. He kept his eyes closed and listened, to wind in the pines and the occasional phrase of music that floated out of the opened windows of his father's attic studio, a string of piano notes the wind caught and carried away. Then, gathering his resolve, he sat up to unwrap Jon's T-shirt from his knee. The joint was puffy but — he poked a finger at it and then tentatively bent it, straightened it — it seemed OK, considering. What would he have done without Jon, he wondered, in general in his life and that day especially.

Sunlight fell over him. He waited without impatience. His mother would be in the library, grading papers or making lesson plans; Jon would hesitate to disturb her, and she would finish what she was doing before coming out to check on Henry.

Eventually Jon emerged from the house and sat across the step from Henry. He passed over the Ace bandage and took back his shirt. "How does it feel?"

"Fine. Not bad at all, considering." Henry wrapped the bandage around his knee, circling the joint above and below with elastic, crossing the bandage over the kneecap for maximum support. His mother came out, carrying the gold-headed cane Henry used on these occasions.

"You don't want the doctor. Do you?" Henry shook his head. "I've put the heating pad and extension cord on the kitchen table."

Henry looked up at her. "Jon got it back in."

Mrs. Marr raised her eyebrows. Tall, slender, his mother looked like a Chapin, with clear, balanced features, the high cheekbones and small mouth, the eyes gray-green under a broad forehead, her brown hair pulled back and twisted into a knot at the back of her head. She looked briefly at Henry, then turned to Jon. "That was clever of you."

"I've been reading first-aid books, and I thought," Jon handed Henry the cane, "I might as well try using what I've read. Theory is one thing, but practical application is the real test, don't you think?"

Mrs. Marr didn't answer. Henry thought maybe she wasn't interested, or maybe she was thinking about something else. "You'll be all right," she told him. "I've got papers to grade." The screen door clattered shut behind her.

"Let me see you stand up, and all," Jon said. "Do you think you'll come into town this afternoon?"

"I'll put heat on it, for a while. After lunch? I have to proofread that history essay first."

"You've finished it, haven't you? Don't bother

telling me, you've got it finished and rewritten and a final draft done."

"And you haven't even thought about it yet," Henry countered, hauling himself up, balancing his weight on the cane. "Some of you people get your A's so easily."

"That's what it's all about, the chosen race. Do you mind? You don't, do you? It's not as if you didn't get A's, too." Jon looked at Henry, considering him. "A parable. The Parable of the Tortoise and the Hare. The king had in his kingdom a tortoise and a hare. The tortoise was a slow, plodding, careful creature, while the hare was agile, quick, brilliant. One day the king set them to a race. The hare tore ahead, running circles around his opponent, leaping up into the air, and generally acting the extravagant fool, while the tortoise went steadily forward, plod, plod. Both of them completed the course, and the king was satisfied."

Henry protested, "That's not a parable, it's a fable. And the tortoise wins."

"Not in my version," Jon said. "I'll see you if I see you." He walked off down the driveway.

Henry watched him out of sight, then limped into the kitchen. There he settled himself at the table, leg propped up on a chair, the heating pad over his knee as he reread the essay. He'd get an A on it, probably, but it was dull, methodical work, nothing interesting to it. Plod, plod. He'd had a couple of ideas about the shifting political structures of nineteenth-century Europe, but he wasn't sure they were defensible and didn't have the resource materials to check them out, so he'd omitted them. Plod, plod. It was a good piece of work, he knew — flawless. Merely flawless. He lowered his leg to the floor, stapled the pages together, turned off the heating pad, and consulted his stomach. It was time for lunch.

His father came into the kitchen and nodded in Henry's direction. After the morning's work, Henry's father walked along the beach. Edwin Marr had a deceptive look of physical strength to him. Henry watched his father move across the room. He wasn't sure whether his father had been greeting him, or nodding at some thought of his own. Henry never knew whether he was supposed to respond to such gestures or not, or, if he was supposed to, what form that response should take.

Toasted peanut butter and jelly, that was what he'd have. Waiting for the toast to pop up, he poured himself a glass of milk. When the toast was ready, he moved efficiently, buttering it, peanut-buttering it, spreading bright jam over one slice and quickly closing the sandwich together, to keep as much heat inside as he could. The first bite was always the best, crunchy toast and soft insides, all permeated with the flavor of peanut butter. He ate standing up at the counter, then cleaned up after himself. He completed the meal with a banana and decided he'd walk the distance into town, and visit Jon. It hurt to move the knee, but not that much. It was probably good for him to work the joint.

Henry went by the road, using the cane as much for balance as support. The road was a longer way than the beach, unless you were using a cane that would dig into the sand at every step. At the town limits, he cut down a dirt road to the harbor. Granite blocks that bulwarked the harbor on three sides gave him stable footing. The only impediments he faced were the huge cleats sunk into the stones at mooring intervals, so he could look around him.

The harbor sheltered a shrinking fishing fleet and growing numbers of charter boats, which during the season would be out all day long, seven days a week, along with rental rowboats, all of them green, which were available by the day or the hour to tourists who wanted to spend some of their vacation time on the water. Pairs of markers, black and red, lined the passage from the harbor out to sea. On the second marker, Henry saw an osprey nest. The deeply anchored marker rose up on three metal legs above the waves and the nest had been built on the platform underneath a red triangle. Henry scanned the sky and shoreline, but couldn't see the birds, neither circling above nor perched on a high tree to catch the movement of fish underwater and dive — talons as large as a man's hand and three times as strong extended. Only the untidy nest testified to their presence.

He looked ahead to his destination, Leo's, on the other side of the harbor. To get there, he made his careful way across the broad stones. Barnacles grew up the sides of the granite blocks and seawater stained them yellow. Slime covered them as high as the water could reach. The waves ran up against the flat wall, sending up a fine spray, making the surface slippy.

He had to use his hand to lift his bad leg over the low fence that separated the restaurant lawn from the vacant lot next door. Mr. Nafiche had established his restaurant in an abandoned chandlery and, in summer, tables were set out on the lawn, with umbrellas opened over them during the day and candles burning in tall glass holders at night. Henry went up the empty lawn to the kitchen entrance, to find Jon. Leo's was a family business. Mr. Nafiche split his time between kitchen and dining room; Jon's job was in the kitchen; his mother baked the strudels and cheesecakes upstairs. Enid, whose vocation was singing, was excused from work except during the height of the season. The Rabbi was always excused, because his vocation was God.

The restaurant kitchen was a large room, with a long wall of ovens, burners, and overhead broilers, paralleled by a long central work area. Sinks, the dishwashing machine, and refrigerators were at the opposite end from the double doors that swung quietly open and closed when waiters entered and left the room. During the season, the kitchen was a welter of activity, but that spring afternoon it was quiet. Across the room from the screen door Henry closed behind him, Jon was tasting chowder: He sniffed over the pot, dipped a spoon in, and sipped at it, bent his head to one side, and then reached up to the shelf above for the whiskey bottle. He poured some whiskey into the soup, stirred, and looked up to notice Henry. Jon raised two fingers — Henry nodded and inhaled deeply. All the smells made him hungry for the taste of food in his mouth, and the substance of it in his stomach. He listened to the quiet voices, the clang of pots, the rush of water. Jon took off the apron he'd been wearing and joined Henry. "They're out front," he said.

The boys walked around outside, to the front entrance. They found Jon's parents seated at a table apart from the few that were occupied, talking intently. Mr. Nafiche's fingers curved around his wife's smaller hand. The two faces looked up. "Henry," Mr. Nafiche said, half rising to shake Henry's hand. "It's good to see you." At their approach, Mrs. Nafiche stood up with a rustle of fabric. "You'll be coming upstairs?" she asked, and left them.

"In a couple of minutes," Jon told her. "I think I'm finished in the kitchen, Pop."

"That's good then. Henry, have you gotten permission for the summer work?"

"Not yet, sir."

"There's plenty of time yet. And what is it

you two have planned for the afternoon?" Mr. Nafiche had a round head, a round face, and thinning gray hair; his usual expression was one of weary eagerness.

"The usual," Jon said. "Some strudel and then who knows. I've got a history essay to write."

"That's good then," Mr. Nafiche said. "Your mother is waiting for you. Is something wrong with your leg, Henry?"

"No, not really."

A long flight of wooden stairs led up the side of the building to the apartment where the Nafiches lived, on the principle, Jon had explained to Henry, of keeping one's family life separated from one's family business. Or, he had added, on the principle of joining them together. It could, he concluded, be either one. The apartment occupied three stories, connected by an indoor staircase. The empty rooms on the third floor were sometimes occupied — by a waiter or cook who had no other place to live, by recent immigrants who needed somewhere for temporary sanctuary on their way to wherever they would settle, Wisconsin or California, Canada or Israel. The Nafiches lived on the first floor — three bedrooms, a bath, and one large room used for kitchen and dining room and living room all together. Between those two was the floor where the Rabbi had his bedroom, large study, and private bathroom, a dignity that befitted his age and his patriarchal role in the family. The Rabbi was Mr. Nafiche's father-in-law, the father of his first wife. She had died, leaving her husband with three children whom his in-laws had helped him raise. When Mr. Nafiche had remarried and moved out to Cape Cod to open his own restaurant, his widowed father-in-law had come with them, along with his adolescent grandchildren and the young children of his son-in-law's new wife. Jon thought of the Rabbi as a grandfather; and he was, in fact, the nearest thing to a grandfather Jon had.

They entered the kitchen from a narrow hallway. The Nafiches' kitchen was almost as large as the one downstairs, with a large wooden table at its far end, set around with unmatched wooden chairs. Mrs. Nafiche was at the stove, pouring hot water into a drip coffeepot, brewing a pot of tea for Henry, who didn't like coffee. She had set a long golden strudel out on the table, with knife, plates, and forks beside it. Along the high walls, open shelves were crowded with boxes and cans of food, with bowls and cutting boards, with plates and glasses. A row of high windows at the back of the room let light in. Henry went to his usual seat while Jon and his mother brought coffee, tea, milk, sugar, and cups. "Did you walk — excuse me, hobble, into town?" Jon asked, sitting down.

Henry nodded.

"I'll ride you back, OK?"

"You don't have to."

"C'mon, Hank, you knew I would. I just thought I'd spare you the effort of constructing a whole lot of subtle hints."

"I don't know why you let him pick on you like that, Henry," Mrs. Nafiche remarked, sitting down next to Jon. She gave Henry his teapot and a cup, then poured coffee for herself and Jon. Henry thanked her. Mrs. Nafiche had eyes like Jon's, speaking eyes, only hers glistened with tears that were always near the surface. Mrs. Nafiche wept when she was sad or happy, wept when she was worried or pleased, wept when she was angry. A plump woman, her skin glowed with beige tones. Her features were too heavy and irregular for beauty, her mouth too full, her eyebrows dark and uneven; and she was the most beautiful woman Henry had ever seen. She dressed in full blouses and skirts, to disguise all the extra pounds, she said. Her clothing flowed around her, in deep colors, rose and green and gold. "You'll have a piece of my strudel?" She cut it for Henry before he had even said Yes, thank you.

"Tell me, what happened to your leg?" she asked. "Did you fall off your bike? You can eat, can't you? Is it your ankle? You've seen a doctor, haven't you? Jon, you should have told me. Does it hurt very much, Henry?" Her eyes filled with sympathetic tears. "Well, is either of you going to answer me? Pass Henry the sugar, Jon. You should know he takes sugar, after all these years you should remember and he can't very easily

46

get up and come around to get it for himself. Why didn't you tell me?"

"I thought Henry might like to surprise you," Jon said. Mrs. Nafiche puffed out her cheeks in mock exasperation. "Good strudel, Ma."

Henry mumbled agreement, his mouth full. Apples and raisins and the thin crisp dough — it was the strudel he always had on Sunday afternoons at the Nafiches', and the first bite was always particularly good. He swallowed and said, "It's wonderful."

"You always say that," she told him.

"And he always means it," Jon said. "And he's always right."

She reached over to rest her fingers on Henry's wrist, briefly, then put her hand on Jon's shoulder. Jon caught it and held it, briefly. Her eyes moistened but she put a bite of pastry firmly into her mouth, and chewed. "What *did* happen?"

"My kneecap went out of joint."

She looked at Henry, who had no more to say, then turned to her son.

"That's what we mean by New England reticence. I'll tell you about it, Ma. He fell down a sand dune, because we were racing. I was ahead, a point that shouldn't be forgotten. But Henry fell. Then, he just lay there, still as death, pale as death, his eyes squeezed closed, like this. 'O what can ail thee?' I asked, 'Alone and palely loitering?' There was a lot of loitering, Ma." Jon took a bite, then took up his story. "So there was Henry clutching his knee with his

47

hands." He demonstrated. "The leg was bent. When he moved his hands away, I could see this kind of huge dimple, where the kneecap was supposed to be, where it should have been and we both wished it still was — and a — a jutting out malformation. Concave socket — the loose bone plate lurching to the side — skin stretched tight over it. It was pretty revolting. The skin especially, for some reason, all distended. Henry sweated, and swore, but he didn't complain. It was pretty impressive, Ma."

"That's true?" Mrs. Nafiche turned her brown eyes to Henry. He could feel the sympathy in her glance, almost a physical touch, her feeling for what he had endured and how he had endured it. He knew he was blushing. "This is what happened to your knees when you were — it was seventh grade, wasn't it? Shouldn't you be lying down, resting it?"

"Jon didn't say, but he's the one who got it back in. The kneecap."

Mrs. Nafiche insisted that Henry explain, in detail. Throughout the recital, she looked back and forth between them, alternating sympathy for Henry with pride in Jon, and vice versa. Her eyes filmed with tears. She asked questions and didn't listen to the answers.

As this extended drama neared its conclusion, Jon's grandfather entered the kitchen. Although Henry thought of the craggy old man as the Rabbi, he never addressed him by the familiarity of a name of any kind. The Rabbi disliked him,

48

and didn't pretend otherwise. Jon had once told Henry the Rabbi's life story — a brilliant Yeshiva student, in Philadelphia, a follower of the ethical moralist Hermann Cohen and an advocate of reform, the events of the thirties and forties, especially but not exclusively the Holocaust, had led him to turn his mind and life to the Torah, and his back to the world. "How can a Jew live in this world?" Jon had asked Henry. "And remain a Jew," he'd added, before Henry could say anything.

The Rabbi sat down on Jon's other side. He accepted a glass of tea saturated with sugar and declined the serving of strudel that was set in front of him. The Rabbi always wore heavy black suits, with the four long tassels of his undervest hanging down from under the jacket; he had a pale bony face, pale brown eyes, and an impatient mind. "So. You are here again," he said to Henry, but his attention was on the strudel, which he picked at with his fork, as if examining the flakiness of the pastry, the succulence of apples and raisins, the sweetness of nuts. He ate it, as if accidentally.

"Yes, sir."

"You celebrate no Sabbath."

"You'll never convert Henry with that attitude," Jon told his grandfather.

"Convert?" The old man put a chunk of strudel into his mouth, but not as if he was eating it. "Pah," he said. "I begin to think that when The Day comes, these converts will be no better

49

than the gentile nations to the eye of the Shechinah, blessed be his name."

"It's the flames of Gehenna for you," Jon translated for Henry. "But Rabbi, was not Jonah sent to Ninevah?"

The light brown eyes narrowed. The Rabbi put a raisin into his mouth and closed his teeth upon it.

"And were not," Jon asked, "the sailors on Jonah's ship saved?"

"If the Master of the Universe is merciful, that is beyond our understanding," the Rabbi countered.

"How are we to understand it, if the Master of the Universe is merciful?" Jon asked. "Are we not made after the image?"

"He used to say," the Rabbi said, "*And he that puts the crown to his own use shall perish.*"

What crown, Henry wondered; who used to say? It sounded like the Bible.

"As it is written," Jon said at last. "*Should I not spare Ninevah, that great city, wherein are more than six score thousand persons that cannot discern between their right hand and their left hand; and also much cattle.*"

The Rabbi nodded his head up and down, and said, "Pah." The argument was concluded.

"So," Mrs. Nafiche asked Henry, "what do your parents say? Can you work for us this summer?"

"I haven't had a chance to ask yet."

Mrs. Nafiche was puzzled by this, and Henry

could understand why. The Nafiches brought up whatever was on their minds the minute they set foot in this room, and whoever happened to be around gave advice or made decisions. Jon once told Henry that if the kitchen was empty you just talked to yourself and gave yourself the best advice you could; that the discussion preceding decision didn't require more than one participant. Henry almost believed him.

"I think I'll be able to ask them tonight," he said.

"We would watch over you carefully," Mrs. Nafiche assured him. "You can promise your mother that."

"Promise his mother what?"

Henry turned around.

"Don't bother telling me, I probably don't want to know." Enid's eyes glanced over at Henry, cool blue, uninterested blue. He kept his eyes on her, not letting her abash him, which was easy now. As long as it wasn't love, lust could almost be an aesthetic pleasure, he thought. She didn't greet him. "Cut me a slice of strudel, will you, Jon?" Enid leaned over her mother's shoulder to pour coffee, then sat down at the head of the table. "Did you tell him?" she asked, pulling the plate of strudel toward her. "Did you?" she insisted, lifting the fork. "Then I will. If nobody else has." She looked at Henry. "We're taking in another stray."

THREE

"Not a stray, he is your cousin," Mrs. Nafiche corrected her daughter.

Henry turned to Jon, to ask the question.

"Among the Jews, there is no stranger," the Rabbi pronounced.

"The Jew is always a stranger," Enid said. "There's nobody in this room that's not a stray — except maybe Jon."

Henry turned to Enid, to ask what she meant. She glared at him, blue intolerant eyes in porcelain skin.

"You don't understand," Mrs. Nafiche said.

"Mother, I understand too well. I don't mean anything by it. I only asked if anyone had told the news to our little gentile stray."

Mrs. Nafiche did. "My younger sister's child,

David Steintodt, twenty years old." Her dark eyes glistened.

"You have a nephew?" Henry thought all of Mrs. Nafiche's relatives had died in what he had at last learned to call the death camps. "How did you find him?"

"Six years ago — wasn't it?" Mrs. Nafiche asked the Rabbi, who nodded agreement. "A boy then, fourteen he weighed sixty-six pounds. He'd been living in the displaced persons camp. He was — the doctors said he would need special care, special treatments — he didn't want to eat, he couldn't sleep. Nobody knew how to help him."

"Now he comes home to us." The Rabbi glared at Henry.

"But how did he survive?" Henry asked Jon.

Mrs. Nafiche answered him. "We think, because he turned up in Bavaria, that my sister must have sent him to live with the girl who was the nursery maid. David remembers nothing of those years, he can tell us nothing, but I know the girl had come from the south, I remember she was a rustic."

"We think," Jon explained, "that he must have been sent to stay with her family. Because he turned up there."

"Were you looking for him?" Henry asked. He'd never heard anything about this David. Jon had never said.

"We knew what had happened to all the others," Mrs. Nafiche said. Her eyes wept. "He was the only one we'd been unable to learn anything of. So there was hope. We didn't expect to find him, it was only hope, and we put papers on record with all the agencies, if they should come across him."

"He knew no law," the Rabbi added. With his age, the Rabbi's skin had shrunk so that his face seemed carved from stone, the bones and long furrows and deep eye sockets. "He knew nothing, neither how to read nor write, who he was, where he was, among whom. They didn't even leave him his name."

Jon leaned forward to tell the story. "See, originally he was brought into the camp by Americans. Germany had surrendered, long since, and he came screaming out at a patrol — he's probably lucky he wasn't shot — screaming in German out of the bushes or whatever. That his name was David, not Ulli, that's what he was screaming. Who knows why? So they brought him in with them. From there, he was taken to the DP camp."

"Fourteen years old and he weighed sixty-six pounds. How he had lived, like an animal," Mrs. Nafiche said.

"He's alive," Enid pointed out.

The others, Henry knew, were not. Only Mrs. Nafiche, a young widow with two small children, had been willing to risk a proxy marriage to an unknown man, so that her passport would be American and she could leave Germany. She hadn't been able to persuade the others of the necessity.

"He's going to live with us," Enid told Henry, like a challenge. "The doctors say it's all right for him now."

"That's good, isn't it?" Henry asked. He didn't know what he should say. "Because he must be better now. What was wrong with him?"

"Psychiatrists," Enid said.

"He remembered his name, and nothing more, not even his mother. My sister, Sofie — we don't know — where she was taken — when she died — only, that they were rounded up with — " Her voice collapsed. The Rabbi put his hand over hers, and held tight. Mrs. Nafiche wiped her eyes with the back of her free hand. Henry passed her his paper napkin.

"She has saved her son, and he comes home to us," the Rabbi said to Mrs. Nafiche. She blew her nose, smiled, and wept. The Rabbi looked to Henry, as if there was something Henry should say.

"But what does it have to do with me?" Henry asked Enid.

"He'll be a member of the family," Jon explained.

Enid pushed back her chair and left the room. A minute later, Henry heard the sound of her piano, the notes so precise and implacable in their progress that he guessed they were Bach. Everyone at the table sat listening.

"That sounds like pretty good news to me," Henry said at last. But if it was such good news, why were they all acting so weird?

Mrs. Nafiche gave him a watery smile. She clutched at the sodden napkin. Henry fetched her a box of tissues from the shelves, careful not to limp.

"He will go to the high school, as a senior," she told Henry. "Everything is arranged."

"When's he coming?" Henry asked. If David was twenty, wasn't he too old for high school? Unless, because of those lost years, he was way behind.

"Soon." She blew her nose, wiped her eyes again, and this time her smile reached into her eyes. "He will live upstairs, with the Rabbi, so that he'll have his privacy and yet not be alone."

They were all silent again, for several minutes. Henry had no idea what everyone else might be thinking — he was wondering why David had been kept such a secret. He wondered what was wrong with David, that they'd kept him so quiet; he wondered what was wrong with himself, that Jon hadn't told him about David. If it hadn't been for Enid bringing it up, when did Jon plan to tell him? Jon would have good reasons, he knew, and he knew it didn't really have anything to do with him, David didn't. Jon didn't tell him everything, there was no law that said Jon had to tell him everything, was there? The melody wound around itself, entwined itself in itself, some complex set of variations on a single theme.

Mrs. Nafiche enclosed her coffee cup with both hands, and stared into it. "Ma?" Jon put an arm around her shoulders. "What're you thinking?"

"Not what you guess," she answered, teasing him. "It's nothing like what you are guessing it is. I was thinking about Saul. About the king, Saul. Because of Jonathan, and David."

Jon shifted in his seat and watched his mother's face. "What about Saul?"

"Oh — how he loved his son . . . and how it must have eaten at his heart like bitter herbs — "

"I think I'll change my name," Jon said. "Not that I'm superstitious, but a stitch in time, as it is written."

His mother laughed and reached over to hold his hand. "And what would you change your name to, if you could."

Jon had the answer ready. "Solomon. That's modest enough, isn't it? It's still in the royal line, but at a more fortunate time in the history." His glance included Henry in the joke. Henry grinned back at Jon. "And with luck, there might be a Sheba in my future."

"I think you've gone far enough," the Rabbi said.

"I'm sorry," Jon said, sincerely, then changed the subject. "Is it OK if I ride Henry back to his house?"

"Yes, of course," Mrs. Nafiche said, "but why so soon?"

"I've got an essay due tomorrow."

Mrs. Nafiche reached out her hand to Henry, not to actually touch him, just to reach out. "You take care of your knee, and come again, soon."

"I will," Henry assured her of both. He nodded at the Rabbi, who didn't respond. Jon handed him his cane and led him out of the room.

Henry sat on the seat of the bicycle, one hand holding his injured leg steady, the other gripping onto Jon's belt. Jon braced the cane across the handlebars, and pedaled, and complained. He didn't say anything about David, and Henry didn't ask. Jon puffed dramatically and inquired about Henry's recent weight gain. He cited instances of boys their age who had had heart attacks. He made invidious comparisons between the uphill grades on the road, and the Alps. "You've never even seen the Alps," Henry pointed out, and didn't ask anything about David.

Jon turned the bike around to go right back. What's wrong with everybody? Henry wanted to ask — except you and your father — what is it? Jon mounted the bike, one foot on the ground, and looked down to the end of the driveway. He took a breath and said, "He's not cured. David."

"It must be OK if they're letting him out."

"I guess so. As it is written: Time will tell."

"What's he like?" The words were out before Henry could stop them.

"I have no idea. They never let me go with them when they visited the hospital, and they never said. You know how they are — they talk a lot but some things they never mention at all."

Now that Jon was back to normal, Henry wasn't worried. "There's probably a good reason."

"Hank, if I told you my mother cooked with ground glass, you'd tell me she must have a good reason. And so would Pop. She's had her heart set on having him, David, as long as I can remember, from the first."

"I can see why."

"So can I," Jon agreed. He raised himself onto the seat. "Think of me later, as you roll into bed for a good night's sleep and I'm slaving away." He rode away, down to where the driveway joined the road, and turned left without stopping.

At supper, Henry interrupted the silence to tell his parents about David Steintodt, not because he thought they would be interested, but because he wanted to ask about the summer job. "A cousin of Jon's is going to come live with them," he said. "He's Mrs. Nafiche's nephew, from Germany."

"Didn't you tell us she lost her whole family in the concentration camps?"

"Death camps," Henry said. Both of his parents looked up, but said nothing.

"I asked a question," his mother pointed out.

"Yes, I guess I did." Well, it was what Jon had told him. "I didn't know."

"They must be nice people. There's nothing else they could have done, but still it's generous of them to give him a home," Mrs. Marr said.

"Mr. Nafiche asked me to work in the restaurant, a summer job. In the kitchen. Afternoons. If you let me take it," Henry said, "I'll need a social security number."

"If you take it, you'll have to stick with it," his mother warned.

"I will." She should know that about him.

"How many hours will you work?"

"Four hours a day, five days a week including weekends, which are the busiest times."

"You'll have to take a week off, in August, when we visit your grandmother."

"I told Mr. Nafiche and he said that was fine."

"Then I guess you have our permission. You'd better open a savings account at the bank."

"I was going to give the money to you."

"Why should you do that?" his mother asked.

For household expenses — food and clothing, gas for the car — for whatever, Henry thought of saying, for any of the things there is never enough money for. He put his fork down and waited for his parents to finish, then cleared the table, and ran hot water into the dishpan. While he washed glasses, plates, utensils, and pans, they drank coffee, each lost in thought.

David crept back into his mind, as he rinsed and dried and put away. You'd have thought, he thought, that the Nafiches would be excited, and glad. After all, David had survived.

FOUR

Thinking about David, Henry felt himself being drowned in pity, a feeling that flowed up and over him, carrying him helplessly along. If David was twenty now, he'd have been three, four, something like that, at the start, a little child; but not so young as to be unknowing. Just too young to defend himself in any way. Six million was an unimaginable number; but one — Henry could imagine one, and if it was almost more than he could bear, helplessly sinking into pity, he wondered how David stood it. The fact of David stood out, like the isolated figure of the man picked out by fate.

He didn't say any of that to Jon, just as he never did ask why David had been kept such a secret. If Jon didn't want to tell him, that was Jon's business. Besides, he couldn't because Jon wasn't often there to ask questions of. He dropped out of baseball, which Henry continued with. This was the week Jon came to school with paint on his shoes, paint crusting his fingernails and dusting his hair. He was repainting David's room, white walls (Monday and Tuesday) and blue woodwork (Wednesday, Thursday), because his mother had decided white and blue were better colors for David than the sand and brown they had previously painted the room, getting it ready for David. Henry offered help but Jon declined it. "You'll need varsity letters, at least one, if you want to apply for an ROTC scholarship. They like athletes in the military, don't they? Do you know about ROTC scholarships?" Henry didn't, so Jon explained and then asked, "Will you go into Cambridge with me next Saturday, to get books for David?"

"On Saturday?" They were eating lunch. Henry picked his way through a thin slice of cafeteria meat loaf while Jon chomped away at a thick cheese and tomato sandwich. Jon reached into his paper bag and brought out two large pieces of cake, one of which he passed over to Henry. "Ma sends you this. Don't you want to?"

"But isn't it the Sabbath?"

"The Rabbi gave permission, because it's for David."

"Why not ask Enid? She's in Boston already."

"She's all tied up with work and doesn't even expect to get home again until her exams are over. They'll make her though, probably — I think. To meet David. You haven't said yes or no, Hank. Don't you want to? I want you to want to. It's our treat, Pop said I had to make that clear, because you'd be doing us a favor."

"Of course I do," Henry said. "I'm just surprised is all."

Jon didn't say anything.

So they took the early morning bus from Hyannis into Boston, and Jon put Henry beside the window — "For when you feel carsick, Hank" — and then diverted Henry's attention by telling the long story of his parents' marriage — "Marriage and courtship, in that order." How Marya Rosen, widowed mother of two, had married by proxy, she in Köln and he in Yonkers, one Leo Nafiche, a widower with three children of his own; how she had brought her children across the ocean and debarked in New York to meet the husband whose citizenship enabled her to leave Germany. "I don't think either one of them expected to fall in love. Pop is much older than she is — like your parents, do you ever think about that? And there were all of these kids, his and hers, too. But they did, and moved to Eastport to open the restaurant, and had me — which was, of course, the point of the whole thing. How're you holding up, Hank?"

They took the MTA over to Cambridge, to go to the Harvard Coop. The first few books were easy to select: a copy of Plutarch's *Lives*, Modern Library editions of *Crime and Punishment*, *War and Peace, Pride and Prejudice*, Sherlock Holmes, Chekhov. "I've always wanted to read Chekhov," Jon said. He led Henry to the foreign language shelves and sat him down before the few choices of Hebrew texts. "But I don't know anything about it," Henry protested. "Not Hebrew, or how to teach languages."

"That's right." Jon stood, looking down, not influencing Henry in any way. "You *have* to pick it, Henry. The Rabbi said so." The Rabbi's word was law.

While Henry looked through the choices Jon talked on. "Everybody's efforts since we found him have been spent straightening David out, or something. He's never even celebrated the High Holy Days, never mind the Sabbath. God knows what he's eaten."

"I thought," Henry looked up at Jon's broad, laughing face and continued, "that if you were Jewish — that being Jewish was the most important thing about you. How come David has been neglected?"

"I think when he went into a hospital the best one Pop could find wasn't Jewish. Probably Episcopalian, what do you think? Anyway, once you start a treatment it's better not to switch. Didn't you ever have any crazy relatives? No," Jon answered himself, "of course not. What am I thinking. There are no crazy Chapins, just stable, self-disciplined, salt-of-the-earth Chapins."

"But," Henry insisted, "I'd think that if David was . . . unstable, it would be good for him to know about Jewishness. The laws and traditions. Because they're so strict and all, it would be secure, wouldn't it?"

"I'm not going to argue with you about that. But I'm not the doctor and neither do I pay the bills. Parable." Henry put back one text and pulled out the next. "Let's see." Henry flipped through the pages, looking for the first lesson. "The Parable of the King with the Blind Son." Henry put the book on the floor beside him and reached down for his last alternative. "Once there was a king whose seventh son was born blind. The king sent him into another country to learn Braille, because his own kingdom had no knowledge of it. The other sons criticized their father for this, saying that the brother would be better in his own home, in his own country. The king answered that in his own country the boy would learn nothing at all. But when the boy returned from his sojourn among strangers, he could barely converse in his native tongue, and he kept running into walls and furniture when he tried to move around the palace. So his father had to send him back to live in the foreign land, and there he married and begat sons who were not blind."

Henry passed Jon the text he'd chosen. "What is that supposed to mean?" He wondered if the Nafiches expected David not to be Jewish after all, whatever his birth.

"I'm not sure," Jon said. "What else?" he asked, as Henry stood up. "We've got enough money left for a couple more books."

"What about *The Federalist Papers*, for American History."

"David's had his fill of history," Jon said. "History is what's wrong with him. How about Thurber?"

"Or Hemingway?"

"Or both?"

When they had settled themselves onto the uncomfortable bus seats for the long ride home, Henry once again next to the window and fresh air, Jon asked, "Your uncle went to Harvard, didn't he?"

"Until the war. He was in the law school, first year, when Pearl Harbor came. That's what Chapins are, doctors and lawyers."

"Except you."

"Except me," Henry agreed, pleased with himself.

"And your father. Did he go to college?"

"In New York, some place called Juilliard. It's a music school."

Jon stared at him. "You don't know from nothing, Hank. Juilliard is *the* conservatory. Best, most competitive. Number one. If I were your father, I'd take a strap to you."

"He's a pacifist," Henry pointed out.

"The world needs more of those."

"Are you serious?"

"I don't know, am I? Maybe I am. Do you know, Henry, the sixth commandment in Hebrew reads, 'Thou shalt not murder.' Murder, not kill; the Christians changed it to kill. What do you think about that? Because it follows to reason that all true Christians should be pacifists, not to mention vegetarians, not to mention that the Spanish Inquisition should never have taken place. In which case, the strong men of the Western World should be the Jews. Ergo, the Chosen People should be the master race. So that, further, history proves how mankind has strayed from God's plan. What will He do about that, I wonder. And when?"

Henry's mind moved more slowly over the idea. "But that assumes man has comprehended God's intention."

"The flaw in my thinking, precisely. That's why the Rabbi likes you."

"He doesn't like me."

"That's nothing personal. He dislikes all gentiles. But he keeps telling me what a serious boy you are, which is a great compliment. He thinks I'm flighty."

"Jon? Why *did* Enid say that about strays, say it that way?"

"Native meanness, maybe. Or maybe — she says we could have things easy if Pop didn't give so much money away, to Israel, to David, then Ma wouldn't have to work."

"I thought your mother liked cooking."

"My mother likes my father, and anything to do with him. If he were a tailor, she'd polish his needles. If he were a judge, she'd read law. Maybe Enid doesn't like owing Pop so much, and in her twisted way nagging is how she thanks him? Maybe she feels guilty."

"Why should Enid feel guilty?"

Jon shrugged. "We all do, any Jew who survived."

"You don't. Do you?"

"Not much. But I'm spoiled rotten — just ask Enid about that."

"What about David, he must, does he?"

"How should I know, I've never met the guy."

Puzzling over, wondering about, David, Henry noticed how little Jon had to say. Jon seemed more interested in Henry's baseball career. "Varsity letters on varsity sweaters look good on college applications," he announced. He egged Henry on, over lunches, talking about the honor of the class of '54, advising Henry to read Kipling and learn to lift weights with his feet. He offered — later, after David came and his mother simmered down — to ride his bike beside Henry while Henry jogged, nothing too ambitious, a good runner could do thirty miles without breathing heavily, think of the Greeks, they were good runners. Which had nothing to do with David.

Henry did learn that the Nafiches were going to drive down to Connecticut on Saturday, to fetch David, but only because he asked Jon about Sunday plans. So much had changed because of David that he couldn't be sure of Sunday and he didn't want to appear unwelcomed on

Jon's doorstep. "That's two Sabbaths in a row I'll have missed," Jon said, passing Henry a piece of crumb-topped apple kuchen. "It's Gehenna for me. Me and the murderers and adulterers, the heathen and pagan and gentile nations. And you, Henry. At least, you'll be there, too."

"Maybe." A vague threat or a vague promise.

Jon refused to take him seriously. "Imagine it: an eternity of losing to me at chess."

"Maybe." Grimly dubious.

"Ah." Jon finished his piece of kuchen and licked his fingers clean. "I can already see the benefits of intermural competition in you — increased self-confidence, yes, and aren't you taller?"

"Up yours." Sometimes Henry got tired of being made fun of, or, of not counting for enough to be told anything.

Jon's face froze in mock horror, but his eyes gave him away. "You're so manly these days. Up mine. Up my what? Up my nostrils, it must be. But what up? What goes up nostrils? Q-tips. Fingers. I don't know, Hank, what did you mean to say to me?"

Henry laughed, sorry he'd opened his mouth. "C'mon. You know."

"Do I? I'm not sure. Tell me Hank. Explain."

Waiting Sunday morning away — for Jon at least, but by this time it was David Henry really wanted to see, to meet and talk to. Just to settle the questions. Although, if Jon had asked, Henry wouldn't have been able to say what the questions were.

Usually Jon came by in the morning. Henry — his homework completed the day before — sat waiting on the porch steps, then jogged up and down the driveway because he didn't like wasting time just sitting around waiting. He made himself a peanut butter sandwich for lunch and then walked along the shore — a quarter mile down toward town, the gray uneasy ocean on his left, the mounded dunes on his right, expecting to see Jon, at any moment, and a stranger perhaps with him; then the quarter mile back up again, listening for a call from behind.

When low clouds finally disgorged their rain, he gave up expecting Jon, and David. He went inside and lay down on the sofa in their seldom-used living room, reading the Sunday paper. The meetings at Panmunjon were stalemated again. They'd never end the war that way, those old men diddling around, alternatively talking and walking out. Wars ended on the battlefield, like Hiroshima or Waterloo — it took a military victory to finally finish Napoleon. He wondered what Jon would say about that theory, and David. Rain drizzled down the windows.

What their house needed was some color. Jon said their kitchen was European. "Everything in its place and a place for everything, and the essentials bare. But your living room, Hank, is unfit for human life, aesthetically unfit for human life. Can there be such a situation, do you think?" Henry agreed with Jon but his parents didn't seem to even notice.

After supper, his mother asked him where Jon was. Henry said he guessed Jon was busy with David, and scraped his unfinished pork chop into the garbage. "You know," his mother said, "if it were you, you'd have wanted to introduce Jon right away." Henry turned on the water. "I'm not saying better or worse, Henry. Just different."

"I hear you, Mom," Henry said. He'd meet David the next morning at school, so he didn't know what she was getting so worked up about anyway.

"What about David, where is he?" Henry asked the next morning, when Jon got off the bus. He had to ask twice before he got Jon's attention; the weather had settled in for a three-day blow. Rain spattered onto the ground. Rain slid down the back of his neck. Jon shook his head and raced to the shelter of the building. Henry ran after him.

At lunch Jon talked about the hospital. "It was somebody's old estate. You wouldn't believe it, Henry, acres and acres, with grass that looks like a golf course. The main building, where he lived, it had a portico, and pillars, and two huge oak doors with carved panels, pictures of saints. The original owner bought the doors in Europe, off a church that was closing down. Or whatever churches do. A ballroom with crystal sconces like diamond necklaces, only they use it for a dining room. I wouldn't mind going crazy if I could live there."

Henry waited. Jon would get around to David eventually. Jon just liked talking.

"Gardens, too, and a swimming pool. It must have been something, to live there. It must have cost them a bundle."

"Who?"

"My parents."

"Well, not anymore."

"Yeah," Jon agreed. "The guy made his money in railroads. Imagine. Maybe I should go into business for a living."

"Why did he move out if he was so rich?"

"I don't know, how should I know? But you're right, he probably went broke. That's the old Chapin dash of cold water, right between the eyes."

"I didn't mean — "

"I know. Listen, I have a theory, you want to hear it?" Henry nodded. "What if, instead of any one omnipresent god meddling constantly in daily life, there were, like, angels, one for each person alive. The spirits of your ancestors or something. Your Uncle William would be yours, for example. To look after you, and keep you out of trouble — which means they'd have to know the future. I hadn't thought of that. Anyway, the Jews would have two or three of these

73

apiece, because with the six million there would be a superfluity of spirits in relation to the number of living Jews. So we'd have remarkably good luck — or so it would seem." He watched for Henry's reaction. "Just think about it, it's only a theory, theories never hurt anyone. Did they? Well, yes, I guess they did. If you think about it. So the whole theory should be scrapped, don't you think? Henry? Are you paying attention?"

Wondering, when later that week David had still not turned up, Henry finally asked Jon why.

"He's getting settled. Ma says. He'll start in a week or so, after Shavuos."

"Shavuos? What's that?"

"It's when we decorate the house with greens, like a late Christmas. Or an early one, depending on your point of view. Shavuos is the fertility festival."

"In spring?"

"Also it celebrates the giving of the Law. You *have* to remember, Hank, it was the famous occasion of my bar mitzvah."

"I wasn't invited," Henry reminded him.

"That doesn't mean you won't remember. You remember when you weren't invited, don't you? I don't know, Hank, as my convert you're going to make a pretty poor showing. On Shavuos you have to stay awake all night — except for the women and children of course — because when God came to Sinai to show himself to the Jews they were all asleep in their tents, because they'd been up late, roistering. So poor old Moses ran around — kind of like Paul Revere; we're not so different after all now that I think of it — telling his people to get out of bed, *fast*. Imagine it." Henry almost could. "So at Shavuos, Jews keep watch all night so should He come again he'd find them ready."

"The Messiah?"

"I guess. David doesn't know anything about any of this. The Rabbi is horrified — he's starting David on Hebrew right away, poor guy."

"Poor guy?" Maybe now Jon would say something about David.

"The first year, it's incredibly hard, and boring. Let me demonstrate. Do you have a piece of paper?"

Picking up information piecemeal, that's what Henry was doing. But he didn't know what Jon was thinking. *And* he didn't know what Jon was thinking.

He heard that Enid had come home for David's first weekend, and that she had said she would return on Friday, for the next. "But I thought she didn't have time for anything," Henry said.

"She's got time for David. You jealous, Hank?"

"What have I got to be jealous of?"

"Not David, that's for sure."

Henry wondered what that meant.

"He sits and listens to her practice."

"She never let us do that."

"But we never wanted to." Henry conceded the point. "So, are you jealous?"

Henry considered, and shook his head. "Does lust just disappear?"

"How should I know? I'm *virgo intacto*, an innocent bud in the Garden of Eden, you know that."

Henry stopped expecting David to show up at school, but he couldn't stop himself from wondering. Why David hadn't started, why Jon didn't say. Mrs. Nafiche took David into Boston, to buy clothes and to pick up Enid, so that the one time Henry went home from school with Jon they had the kitchen to themselves. The Rabbi, Henry heard, had decided to give up the Hebrew lessons because David was having so much trouble with them. "Which is funny," Jon said, "because he's so smart. Not just smart, probably brilliant. It might be easier on him if he wasn't."

Henry had to finish chewing, and then swallow, the bite of honey-nut roll that was his share of the snack he and Jon were having outside, on the grass by the harbor, because it was a fine, warm, sunny day. "What do you mean?" he asked.

"I mean smart, like, lots of brains."

That wasn't what Henry had meant, but he didn't insist. "If that's true, then why do your parents want him to go to high school? rather than college."

"They think it'll be good for him to meet people, and going to school with them is a good way. I met you at school, didn't I?"

Henry wanted to meet David just so he could get it over with, and get back to his own life. He was spending too much time wondering when he was going to meet David.

By the fourth Sunday, Henry knew better than to hope. He almost hoped, but he knew better. Through the long morning, he did homework, and he knew he was hanging around hopefully; but in the afternoon he wrapped his knees with Ace bandages and headed down to the beach. To run wind sprints.

As he came over the top of a dune he saw three figures walking along the sand, beyond the water's reach. The wind blew at their backs, molding his father's shirt against his broad back and skinny arms, blowing Jon's dark hair. The third figure, barebacked, his trousers blowing against his legs, must be David. Blond, barefoot, that was what Henry could see.

The wind whipped at Henry's shirt and whipped his hair around his eyes. So probably Jon and David had met up with his father on the beach, which meant that Jon and David had been out walking, which was probably what they did in the afternoons — while Henry was at baseball practice, or at a game.

Henry stood still, and watched them walk away. He shrugged his shoulders, against the wind, and then made his way down the dune side. He wasn't about to kid himself. He was through making such a big deal out of David, and it didn't make any difference, anyway, what he did, or thought.

He sprinted up the packed sand, heading away from town, away from the three of them, running as hard as he could into the blowing sand that cut like little knives.

FIVE

One late afternoon in early May, Henry was running along the beach. The tide was low and the sand flats had been warmed by the sun. The air smelled of salt and seaweed. Henry, running, saw two figures stretched out on the public beach and thought to himself that it was cool to be sunbathing, early for tourists, strange to see anyone there at this time of year — when Jon sat up. Jon at least wore a T-shirt and cut-off jeans; the person behind him, lying face down, was wearing just a bathing suit. The person beside Jon had to be David. Henry almost turned around. But Jon saw him and waved, so Henry — who had by then stopped running — approached them.

Jon got up to meet him. David — it couldn't be anyone else — didn't move. Henry saw thick golden hair and a long tanned back that narrowed down to rounded buttocks in the red bathing suit. Long lean legs, also tanned — David seemed to be asleep.

Jon dug a sandy toe into his cousin's ribs. "I know you're faking. You slept until noon, so you can't be asleep now. We've got company, David. It's worth pretending to wake up for — it's Henry."

David rolled over, gathered his legs under him, and stood, in a single movement, like a bird moving into flight. He looked right at Henry.

It lasted only seconds, but — the eyes darkened by hope, the face alight with it — Henry couldn't imagine what David had seen to give rise to such a feeling, or what David might have heard about him; he couldn't understand his own response, a desire to be worth hoping much of which matched the intensity of David's eyes; the long flat muscles of chest and belly, running down into his groin, tightened in anticipation — for how long, he didn't know. David's hope-filled eyes made time measureless. Henry stepped back.

"Jon's spoken of you," David said, his eyes already empty.

"Hello," Henry said, wondering if he should offer to shake hands. "Hello, David." It was just Jon's cousin, just a couple of people meeting each other. "How are you?" he asked, just to be saying anything, but as he uttered the words he thought that that wasn't at all what you should say to someone recently released from a mental hospital. "What are you doing, sunbathing?" he asked. His mind felt thick, stupid. "Isn't it early in the year for sunbathing?"

"It is that," David agreed, "especially if you're reluctant to risk an extra dose of radiation, like the people who were — " he hesitated over the next word, emphasizing it — "lucky enough to survive at Hiroshima."

Henry felt like a jerk; he wasn't sure why. Why didn't Jon say something. "Well," Henry said, just like a jerk, "I'd bet — "

"Have a seat," David said, sitting down himself. He looked off across the distant water. Deep slate-blue eyes, a nose that was just a little crooked, as if it might have been broken, all features in perfect symmetry. It was shocking how handsome Jon's cousin was.

Jon sat down beside David. Henry sat down beside Jon.

"If I could only see the bottom, I wouldn't mind swimming," David said, "but the sense that the water stretches endlessly under you . . ."

Henry knew that terror. "You get used to it," he said.

"Oh? Yes? You can get used to almost anything, can't you?" David asked.

Henry looked past Jon to see what David was talking about, if it was on David's face; David was already turning back to the horizon. Henry could almost see David at five, or six — he must have looked like a Botticelli angel — and pity welled up in Henry, pushing out at his face from inside. How did you make up to someone for what had been done — so viciously — unimaginably; what could the world ever do to erase those years. Nothing, of course, because they had occurred. And nothing could even begin to apologize, or replace, because individuals were irreplaceable. But Henry was so sorry, he was almost sick with sorrow.

"Where are you going?" Jon asked.

"Home," Henry said. "See you." He didn't want Jon to offer to walk with him. Jon should stay with David.

That night Henry dreamed: Henry stood before a high and mild tide, with David beside him. David held onto Henry's hand, trusting him. The waves licked at their feet, at Henry's big bony feet and at David's palm-sized child's feet. It was warm but not sunny, nor dark, just light. They walked into the water, because there was a world down there, the underwater world, which they were going to. Henry knew they could go there. They had no difficulty breathing, no distortion seeing, as they walked along the sandy ocean floor. They were no longer hand in hand, and Henry turned around. David had finished growing up, and he turned his face to Henry, with its beautiful hoping eyes. Henry's breath caught; his bones liquefied. David reached out until his long-fingered hands touched Henry's ribs, and brushed down them — and Henry stood helpless as his body fused all of its separate parts together, and he ejaculated.

Awake, ashamed even before his pounding heart and throbbing organ had subsided, betrayed — Henry didn't even roll over. He didn't understand, unless — Wet dreams he'd had, and enjoyed them, too. "And rightly so," was Jon's comment — but those were women, and never anybody he knew. Just briefly, he let himself remember — and his whole body grew warm, like water flowing over it, the water like fingers — before he made himself forget.

He couldn't have brought himself to tell Jon. His mind and his memory were too occupied by David; he didn't want Jon intruding. Two days later, when David slid onto the bench beside Jon in the cafeteria, Henry concealed his surprise, his almost physical shock, by attending carefully to the meatballs in watery tomato sauce on his plate. David wore khakis, and a striped tie over his oxford shirt, although no jacket. Henry hunched over his plate, looking up at Jon's cousin but not seeing him. David's hands, which he saw clearly, opened up a paper bag and took out lunch.

"What got you up so early?" Jon asked. "Henry," he said, before David could answer, "please don't eat those things."

Henry put down his fork, folded his arms on the tabletop, and greeted David. "Hi."

"I give up," Jon laughed. "I'll share my lunch with you."

"I won't," David said, as his long-fingered hands unwrapped wax paper from two thick sandwiches.

"That's OK," Henry said. "I don't mind."

"Generous of him, isn't it?" David said to Jon. "Hank's the soul of generosity."

David, Henry thought, didn't like him. "Do you really sleep this late?" he asked.

Taking a bite, chewing, taking another bite, David's only response was a nod of the head. He spoke to Jon. "You told me I ought to at least see what the place was like, so I thought I'd cooperate."

"You don't want to go to school," Henry guessed.

David just looked at him out of flat blue eyes. Such a remark deserved no response.

Henry started piling up plates on his tray. "Wait," David said, reaching out so suddenly that Henry drew back. "I'll finish that, and the pudding, too, if you're not going to."

"Sure, but it's pretty awful." It sounded like David wanted him to stick around.

"I don't mind," David said. Henry looked at his eyes, then, to see if David was making fun of him.

"Yeah, but Ma would mind. She'd have a fit if she saw you eating that. No," Jon said, "you're right, she wouldn't. She'd just be glad you're eating. Maybe I should have the fit?"

"I had a dream, Jon," David said, including Henry in the offer. "You want to hear it?"

"You want to tell it?" Jon asked.

"I asked you first."

"You always ask me first," Jon protested. "And if I do ask you first, you always say you didn't dream anything, or you don't remember."

David's attention was now on his second sandwich, with both Jon's and Henry's attention on him. There was something childish about it, Henry thought, but he didn't mind. It was as if David needed to feel everyone's attention on him, as if his appetite for attention — like his appetite for the food that he consumed steadily, sandwiches, pudding, the rest of the meatballs, and a thick piece of yellow cake from his lunch bag — exceeded the normal. Jon played along, so Henry figured that must be what David needed. He guessed he could understand that; it made sense, given David's history.

"Is that a yes or a no, Jon?" Henry asked. Then he wondered if he'd nosed his unwelcome way in again, wanting David to notice him. He shut his mouth.

David launched into speech. "I dreamed I was walking through a village, and a crowd of peasants had gathered around a cart, harnessed to which was an old nag, all skin and bones. The owner of the cart, drunk as a skunk, drunk as a lord, came out of a bar, calling out to everyone that they should come for a ride in his cart. So they piled in, and the owner, Mikolka, that was his name — "

What a strange dream, Henry thought, trying to see it but unable to visualize it, concentrating fully on David. It struck him as a European kind of dream, probably because of the peasants, he thought, and that name, Mikolka, sounded Greek — he forced his attention onto David's dream. Jon, however, started up laughing and Henry wondered what joke he'd missed.

"C'mon," Jon said. "I know how that one ends already. You can't fool me, David."

When David smiled at Jon, Henry thought David was glad he had caught him out. He'd like to have David smile at him like that. David turned his golden head and did. "I fooled Henry, didn't I?"

Henry grinned, acknowledging.

"And besides, it seems appropriate. Have you got any dreams you want to tell us, Henry?"

He shook his head.

"Then tell me," David leaned toward him; Henry waited, caught, "do you masturbate much?"

Henry looked at Jon. He looked around them to see if anyone had overheard. What was he supposed to do? Ask how much was much?

"They tell me," David told him, "it's a common practice, healthy, too. Unless, like certain Indian gentlemen, you come to prefer masturbation to the real thing."

"I've got to go," Henry said. He stood up. He couldn't stand to stay so close to pain. "See you."

"But there's another fifteen minutes," Jon said.

"I've got a test. In Latin." That was the only course he and Jon didn't take together — Jon took French — so Jon wouldn't know better.

"You're lying, Hank."

Well of course he was. "Why would I lie?" Henry asked.

"How should I know? But it's OK with me if you want to. He who lies last lies best, as it is written. Go ahead. We'll see you, OK?"

Henry took up his tray, and nodded, and walked away from the two of them; let Jon and David think what they liked.

David, Henry thought, probably didn't dislike him; David didn't even know him. What Henry dreamed, after all, was his own responsibility; it had nothing to do with David.

But when, a few days later, David once again came into the lunchroom, sat down next to Jon again, and looked at Henry without welcome, Henry thought it had everything to do with David. He wondered why David wore a tie when he came to lunch at school, as if he had somewhere more important to go to next. He wondered if he looked as confused as he felt and if he'd be able to think of anything interesting to say. Jon, too, fell silent and Henry was suddenly jealous of Jon, who saw David daily, whom

David talked to at least as an equal.

"How'd you like to go to Boston?" David asked Jon. "Uncle Leo isn't using the car this afternoon, and he said I can if you come with me."

"I've got school."

"Hook."

"Is it that you're trying to get me in trouble?" Jon asked.

"Henry will cover for you," David said. "Won't you, Henry."

"How?" Henry didn't expect an answer; there was no possible answer.

"Lie. I suspect you're good at lying."

It was meant to be an insult and it felt like revenge.

"Hank? He can't lie his way out of a paper bag. I can't do it, David. Sorry, but — "

But revenge for what? What had Henry done to David?

"Why not?"

"It's against the rules," Jon said.

"Rules are made to be broken," David said. "He," nodding his head in Henry's direction, "can come along, too, if you can't trust him to cover for you."

But that wasn't what Jon meant at all, was it?

"It's worse for Henry, his mother teaches here. Besides, Jews live by the law, that's our job or our purpose or our something. And the law here says: Thou shalt not cut classes."

"What about I come not to break the law but to fulfill it?" David asked. "He was a Jew."

Henry couldn't follow this conversation.

"Ah, but he wore his Jewishness with a difference."

"No Shakespeare, Jon."

"OK," Jon agreed, "no Shakespeare. I don't know what you have against God, anyway."

Henry was surprised at Jon's obtuseness.

"He forgot my name," David said.

"Not demonstrably. A parable — the Parable of the Fences. There was a farmer, who had a herd of sheep — "

David objected. "Why does it always have to be sheep? Why not goats?"

"Cows," Jon said. "A farmer went to market and purchased a herd of cows. When he got home, the first thing he did was build a fence around his pastures. How are we to understand this?"

"He didn't want them to escape," David answered. "He wanted to be able to find them when he had use for them, to milk them or slaughter them. You're being pretty obvious Jon."

"I'm always obvious. Do you mind? I myself find it refreshing."

"Maybe I'll go on my own."

Jon shook his head.

"What's to stop me?"

"Well, you promised for one thing."

"What's to make me keep promises?"

"And you won't have a good time. You want me with you because you'll have a good time if I'm there, because I'm fun to be with," Jon said.

"I'm a lot more fun than you are, David. You can't deny that."

"Yes, I can."

"But it won't be true."

David looked at Henry. "How about you?"

David had to know how much trouble they'd get into. It wasn't worth it.

"OK, be yellow bellies, there's a long tradition for just doing what you're told, following orders, isn't there, Jon? Henry?"

Henry looked at Jon, who grinned and shook his head. "It's the testicular squeeze play, Hank. Specious, David. False analogy. You can't fool us."

David gave up. "Even," he said, "if you admit the possibility of the virgin birth — which I don't, because those classical girls were always going to their fathers and saying that some god had impregnated them, and their fathers at least pretended to believe them — but it wasn't as if there weren't dozens of religious nuts crucified by the Romans. Crucifixion was the Roman way of execution. Christ just had a better PR team than all the rest of them."

Henry wanted to ask about the rest of them, who they were, what they believed, but he didn't want David thinking he was stupid, so he kept his mouth shut.

"Or," Jon said, "there could be a message in it."

"Like what?"

"How should I know, David? Maybe it's a

reminder to keep the law. Maybe it's advice to up-and-coming prophets: Surround yourself with good writers?"

"If what you want is to be immortalized? Maybe, but — those writers were . . . I mean, it may be that stars will fall like figs, but my money is on bombs falling like stars falling like figs."

Henry had no idea what David was talking about, but he knew what he meant. He didn't know anything about figs, either, like where they grew, or what kind of tree, or how they fell.

"What money?" Jon asked. "Have they given you an allowance? They never gave me an allowance. They are, aren't they? How much? Tell me, David."

But David wouldn't tell and Henry — wondering if Jon might be jealous of David — gathered back the tray that David had once again eaten clean, to obey the bell that summoned him to Latin. Jon and David rose at the same time, David saying, "I'll never tell. I promised. Uncle Leo's waiting for me in the car, Jon."

It was only a couple of days after that that David followed Jon down the steps of the school bus. When Henry saw David, he simply smiled. David looked like something out of an advertisement about New York; Henry wondered if he could carry off that kind of style. He had a couple of ties, required for dinners at his grandmother's house, a suit would be too much but he had a jacket. He was tempted. "Good morning," he said, smiling, "are you enrolling after all?"

"No," David said, like a glass of cold water in the face.

Henry trailed behind them, and Jon, speaking over his shoulder, answered Henry's question. "He's just trying it on. Ma arranged it." Henry's eyes were on David's long back, and the way he wore his khakis low on his hips.

David joined them for lunch. As soon as he sat down, three senior girls hovered near the table. David glanced up at them, then looked away. One — after consulting — came forward. "We, I, just want to welcome you," she said. She held her tray out in front of her, and she was pretty, with brown eyes and a brown pageboy and generous breasts; he thought she probably wanted to join them. He moved down on the bench, making room across from David. "You probably don't remember me," she said to David. "I'm in your science class."

David nodded his head.

"Anyway, my name's Bunny, which is pretty dumb for a name, but I guess . . ." She looked over her shoulder at her friends, then said, "I just want to sort of be the welcoming committee. Are you going to graduate this June with us?"

David bit into a thick roast beef sandwich.

"He doesn't know," Jon answered.

"Oh," Bunny said. Her hands shifted around

the edges of the pea green tray. "What are you, friends?"

"How should I know?" Jon answered. "David, are we friends? We're cousins, I know that."

"Oh," she said again, smiling at David, waiting to hear if he would say anything, which he didn't. "Anyway, I really hope you like it here."

David stared at her, expressionless. She returned to her friends.

"Well," Jon said. "Well, well. I can see that you're going to expand my social horizons."

"Not if I can help it." David was watching Bunny move along the tables to find a place to sit. "She's more Henry's type. Isn't she, Henry?"

Henry picked up his fork to find out how bad the chicken à la king was. "Not my type at all," he said, since David waited for him to say something. She'd never look at him twice.

"Oh, yes?"

Henry stared at David. It sounded as if David really didn't like him, personally didn't.

"These people wouldn't be good enough for you?"

"I never said that. I never even thought it. What're you trying to make me into?"

"I do seem to have touched a nerve," David remarked.

"Never mind the pleasures of picking on Henry," Jon said, "tell us how the morning was. How were your classes?"

David shrugged. "You know."

"Who do you have?" Henry asked, searching out chicken chunks from among the peas and pimientos. He didn't ask because he wanted to know; he asked because that was what you did ask.

"Why do you ask?" David asked him.

"I'm interested." Henry put down his fork and picked up the carton of milk.

David encapsulated each of them, elevator shoes for the science teacher, vanity in the drama teacher, lack of preparation in math, "then for English . . ." His eyes assessed Henry. "But that's your mother, isn't she."

Henry nodded. David said no more.

"Your father's a weird one," David said, instead. Henry took a deep breath, about to tell David to lay off, but David didn't give him time to speak. "An artist — and that's a hell of a life, if you're real. I wouldn't mind being an artist. He's real — maybe — for his sins, the poor bastard."

Henry had never thought about his father in that way.

"He wants me to take piano lessons," David said.

"From him?" Jon asked.

David pulled Henry's tray over, and began to spoon up what was left of the sauce and peas and pimientos and strings of chicken meat. "Who else? There'd be no charge."

"Enid would be miserable if she knew that."

"She already knows."

"Are you going to?"

"I don't know. I'm not too keen on it, but he really wants me to."

"Henry," Jon said, as if it had just occurred to him, "don't you have a birthday next week?"

"Friday," Henry said.

"So, are you going to start driving your mother to school?"

Henry didn't know. She hadn't even said anything about teaching him to drive.

"And what are you going to do with your birthday check? His grandmother sends him a check, every birthday. You could take us to the movies," Jon suggested. "To celebrate. We'd be happy to help him celebrate, wouldn't we, David?"

"But I'm taking my parents out to dinner. At Leo's. Didn't your father tell you?"

Jon shook his head. "Is this on Friday?"

"No, Sunday, because he said he wanted to do the cooking himself. I thought you must know."

"I knew," David said.

For a second, Henry could see that Jon minded, and for longer than that Henry minded, for Jon; he didn't know why David couldn't keep his mouth shut for once.

"Then we'll take you out for a celebration, it'll have to be Saturday night," Jon said. "David? Do you want to?"

David must have agreed because on Saturday they did go up to Provinceton, where *A Day at the Races* was playing. David drove the Nafiches' station wagon, fast, up the winding road. Henry sat in the backseat and fought to conceal his nausea. As soon as he got out of the car his stomach settled. In the dark theater, sitting next to David's stillness, Henry struggled to enjoy the movie. Afterward, they stopped in at a diner for ice cream. Henry wasn't hungry and didn't particularly want ice cream, but Jon insisted. They sat themselves in a booth, and ordered.

"You," Jon remarked to David, "are a real wet blanket."

"You should have told me it was a comedy."

"Henry thought it was funny," Jon countered. "I heard you laughing sometimes, Hank, don't bother to deny it."

Henry didn't.

"Laughter," David said, "resteth in the bosom of fools. As it is written."

"Do you really think I'm a fool?" Jon asked, apparently only curious.

"No. Just a clown." David sat beside Jon. Henry faced the two of them across the Formica table. "I'm sure it serves some useful social purpose."

Jon's laughter sputtered and his eyes included Henry in the mirth. "Useful social purpose indeed," he said. "He laughs at my jokes when we're alone — sometimes he does, Henry. But on the whole, you're not much of an audience, David."

"Thank you," David said, and bowed his head to accept the praise.

When the waitress put their sundaes down in front of them — two mounded high with whipped cream, sprinkled with nuts and topped with maraschino cherries, one, Henry's, with just ice cream and hot fudge sauce — David wished Henry a happy birthday. "Sweet sixteen," he added to the waitress, who leaned over the table in a thick cloud of perfume. "And never been kissed. Is that right, Henry?"

Henry wasn't about to answer that. David didn't seem to expect him to, because he smiled up at the woman, at her bright red mouth, and suggested, "You could do something about that."

"David," Henry protested. The waitress laughed, and told Henry to come back in a couple of years. She walked away, still laughing, her skirt swinging. "What are you trying to do?"

"You really mind, don't you?" David's spoon stopped halfway to his mouth. "That's interesting. Because you're really uncomfortable, aren't you?"

"I'm angry," Henry said. He didn't look at Jon who would know better. He met David's eyes, pale and assessing across the table.

"That indicates your unmerited response. She's flattered, Henry, I made her feel attractive, women always like that and they understand a sexual response as testimony to their allure, it gives them a sense of power. But your discomfort — call it anger if you want to — makes me think you're even more repressed than I thought. Is he, Jon?"

If Jon even started to answer that question, Henry thought, he'd bash him one. If he was repressed it was nobody's business but his own, and what could he do about it anyway if it was even so bad.

"How should I know?" Jon asked.

"Jon, here, is innocent, inexperienced, but not repressed. It has to do with upbringing more than anything else," David explained, eating steadily, speaking authoritatively. "Your parents, however, are pretty cold types, they're cold people and I'll bet — when was the last time you saw your mother naked?" He didn't give Henry time to respond. "I wouldn't mind seeing her naked, she's got a terrific ass. Didn't you ever wonder why you're only child?"

"Yeah, Hank, I've always envied you that. Of course, your mother only had the one brother, so she's used to a small family. Now my family is large — does it strike you as overlarge, David?"

But David wasn't to be distracted. "What about your father, did his family have a lot of kids?"

"My father was raised in an orphanage."

"Really?"

"No, David, I made it up." Henry forced himself to swallow a spoon of ice cream.

"That explains why he wanted to marry your mother," David said, scraping his bowl clean. "I wondered about that, what they had in common. Jon says hers is an old Boston family, hoity-toity, is that right? But if she's so well-born, I wonder why she married him. If you don't want your sundae, can I have it?"

Henry pushed the bowl across. All he wanted was to get home, get away from David. Looking at the thick golden hair as David attended to the sundae, Henry could still feel sorry for him. But he didn't want to have to spend time with him. He knew David was attractive, he was handsome, really handsome, but Henry was finding him repulsive, physically repulsive, watching him shovel food into his mouth. Mentally, he thought, David was a mess.

Henry looked at Jon, then, who was also eating, but slowly, as if every bite had a flavor he didn't want to miss any of. He hadn't talked to Jon for an age; he hadn't talked, really talked, to Jon since David arrived. He'd barely seen Jon at all without David.

Driving back, Henry sat in the front seat by the window, for the sake of his stomach. Jon sat in the middle. The tall station wagon swayed around curves, at the speed David was taking them. Henry clutched the door handle. He should have said he wanted to sit in back, or he should just tell David to slow down, but he didn't have the courage, did he? He didn't even have the courage to face this careering journey through the dark night calmly, with the pines rushing by and the headlights picking through the dark; and it was at least reasonably sure that you'd see the headlights of an approaching car so you could move out of the middle of the road. But he was sitting there, frightened. He'd never known what a coward he was. Too much of a coward to speak out for himself, even to tell David to lay off his parents, too much to insist that David drive sanely. Jon seemed relaxed, but maybe Jon figured it was worth it to wreck the car and die, worth it because of David. Or maybe he figured that God would take care of him. Henry sat stiff and endured, staring blindly ahead as the road twisted and turned under the wheels of the car, as the car swayed and surged forward into the night.

Henry didn't see it happen, because his eyes were fixed at the reaches of visibility, but he felt the car lurch to the side and heard the heavy thunk of something striking the car, and saw — turning his head — what might have been something, some small body, flying off behind them. The car sped on.

"What was that?" David asked.

"We better stop and see," Henry said.

"Why?" David didn't even slow down.

"Jon," Henry said.

"I think we have to, David."

David shrugged, jammed on the brakes, maneuvered the car around, and headed back, slowly. "We won't be able to find whatever it was."

"We have to at least look," Henry answered, since Jon didn't have anything to say. He hadn't noted any landmarks, on the wooded stretch of road, and since they were going at a different speed he thought maybe David was right, they wouldn't be able to locate the animal.

As it turned out, there was no difficulty, because the air was pierced by a thin screaming sound. Henry thought David was going to drive on past the shape he barely had time to pick out in the headlights, but David turned the car around again, so that the lights shone on the writhing mass.

Henry got out of the car, and Jon followed him, with David behind them. It was a cat — or what had been a cat — its color concealed by the glare and by blood, an eyeball hanging down over its cheek and its bleeding mouth open, as it screamed. What were they supposed to do? Guts had spilt over onto the road, and there wasn't anything to be done.

"You better put it out of its misery," David told Henry.

"Why me? You're the one who hit it."

"You're the one who is going to be a soldier. You're the killer."

Angry, Henry looked around for a weapon. He didn't think, and he didn't want to. The animal screamed, with a sound that sliced through the darkness, and he thought only of stopping the sound. He stepped into the trees until he found a heavy branch, and then he went back to the cat and raised the branch over his head and — not thinking — brought it down on the animal's head. The shock jolted up his arm, across his shoulders. He hadn't realized how hard he'd brought it down. The branch cracked, shattered. The screaming stopped.

"Hear, O Israel," David said.

"David," Jon protested.

Henry was breathing as heavily as if he'd been running.

"The Lord is our God," David said.

"Shut up, David," Jon said. "Animals don't have souls."

"And you do?" David asked.

Henry went back to the car. He didn't realize until he opened the rear door that he still had the stick. He threw it off into the trees.

Neither of the other two looked at him, or spoke to him, all the rest of the way. Jon at least could have said something, or just turned around to look at Henry, or something. Henry was beginning to remember that the car had maybe lurched to the right, just before the impact, but he wasn't sure. Even if you were crazy you wouldn't deliberately try to kill something, would you? He didn't know, he didn't understand, he was — getting out of the car at the end of the driveway — going to throw up, anyway.

He vomited into the long grass at the roadside,

as if he could rid himself of the whole experience, and David, too. As if he could rid himself of himself, and what he'd done. Raising his head in the darkness, wiping his mouth with the back of his hand, spitting, he thought that he had always used to like himself; he had once really liked himself.

SIX

Henry was at the oars, as usual. Jon sat facing him, his attention on David. Henry nosed the rented rowboat toward the tall marker, then kept it level against the uneasy waves, against the unbalancing weight leaning out from the bow. Halfway out into open water as they were, the sea was choppy.

All three of them wore Mae Wests. They'd promised Mr. Nafiche; he'd practically made a ceremony out of it, before he would agree to take a season's lease on a rowboat for Jon and David. "A couple of feet to the right, Henry," David's voice instructed.

"Row on, MacDuff," Jon commented.

Henry knew without asking that David was facing forward, and meant his own right; he lifted the left oar out of the water, briefly, then set it back in, steadying the boat. Jon, without shifting his attention from David, nodded once matter-of-factly, as if that it was Henry he was nodding at did not in fact matter.

"Two," David's voice said. The boat moved uneasily as he turned around, sat down, leaned forward to report to Jon over Henry's shoulder. "Two."

Henry turned the bow of the boat toward shore and lifted both oars out of the water, simultaneously, then shoved both of his arms out straight, and pulled back. The boat moved strongly ahead. He supposed he could have minded always being the one who rowed, but he was the one who was in good shape, and he rowed well anyway — strongly, steadily, over the water, in the wind, under the generous fall of cool May sunshine.

"They only weigh maybe five pounds full-grown," David's voice said, "but their wingspan can be up to five feet."

"Five feet?" Jon spread out his arms, looked from hand to hand. "Are you sure?"

"Yes," David said. "Of course. Why shouldn't I be, I read about it."

"How long is the incubation period?" Jon asked and then "Can they fly as soon as they're hatched? Or how long is it before they can fly? Is it the kinds of feathers they have that define when they can fly? The word *is* hatched, that's the right word, isn't it? Not born, born means from a living womb, but eggs — I don't think I want to think about eggs."

"Eggs in general?" David asked, having patiently dealt with each of Jon's questions as it came. "Or scrambled eggs, what in fact it is that you're scrambling. Boiled are the ones I don't like to think about cooking, when I think that there is a living creature in the shell. Fried are the ones I don't like to think about eating, now that I think about it, what did *you* mean, Jon?"

Jon just shook his head, some wordless response, then turned to look behind him at the nest spilling out untidily over the edges of the platform, and the sea opening out beyond. Henry rowed on, aiming for the seawall at the end of the restaurant lawn. They kept the boat cleated there, in the quiet harbor waters. They stored the oars under the staircase that ran up to the Nafiches' apartment.

If Henry wanted to see Jon he had to see David and he didn't want to see David. He shoved the oars under the steps and picked up his bicycle from the ground where he had dropped it. If he wanted to see Jon without David — at least until school got out; after school got out he'd be working with Jon, almost every afternoon. But for the present if he wanted to see just Jon — not for anything special but just because it was different when it was just him and Jon, better, it was the way it used to be, good — all he could do was hang around his house late in the afternoon to see if it was Jon who walked David up to the Marrs' for a piano lesson. Mostly it was Enid who accompanied her cousin and then waited around to walk back with him; it was reading period, two weeks for study before a week of exams, so she was at home. David came every weekday for an hour's lesson. Occasionally, it was Jon who walked up with him, or walked up to walk back with him.

Henry didn't turn around to see if anyone was watching him ride away. The truth was that David irritated him. The trouble was that David was Jon's cousin, and living in the same house so they were almost brothers. But the guy made him nervous. Anyone who made you have the kind of dream Henry had had about David, even if it was only once — that was creepy. Also, Henry knew that David didn't like him, despised him was what it felt like; but David always wanted Henry along, with Jon. That was creepy, too. Henry disliked David and never wanted him along, with Jon, which was the normal way to feel.

Then, whenever Henry settled in to simply accept that David made him feel sick, he had to remember that David had been over there for the whole war, even if not in the death camps, and that his whole family had died in the camps. He had to remember that David was Jewish. When Henry remembered, he felt so sorry for David it made him feel sick.

* * *

The last day of school finally arrived, and dragged by. Jon declared a week's vacation. "I need to establish my tan. Nobody can ask us to do anything, all week, just for a week. So, will you go along with that, Hank?" They spent much of the week on the town beach, nearly empty in mid-June, where the grainy sand stretched out in both directions, and the dunes stretched along beside the sand, and the ocean stretched endlessly out before them. David's bobbling crawl left him almost stationary in the water, a problem that Jon assigned to Henry. "This is what leadership is all about, Hank. And we are waiting with bated breath to see how you do. Aren't we, David?"

David stood to mock attention and saluted. Sunlight fell over him, like a spotlight. Except that he was wearing a bathing suit he looked perfect, in the military sense, tall, trim, alert, well-muscled — a face that drew your eyes like a magnet. Henry looked to Jon for help. "Does he want to?"

"To improve? Of course. Everyone does." Jon turned to include David. "Don't you, David?"

David studied Henry for a while before answering, "Is it an improvement to be more like Henry?"

"How are we to understand this question?" Jon queried.

Henry cut across the crap. "I think the trouble is your kick."

"Who cares?" David asked. "Who needs to

be able to swim as well as Henry? I can't change my kick, anyway, it's ingrained. It's habit. It's part of me."

They were more successful in teaching him how to ride waves in, on inflated rafts or using his own body if the surf was high enough. Henry admired David sometimes. He dealt boldly with the water and recklessly with his body. He tumbled in on the breaking waves like a jellyfish, or a clump of buoyant seaweed. Once, Jon and Henry had to run down and drag David free of the water. Jon accused David of doing it to show off. Henry didn't point out that they were alone on the beach, because Jon sounded genuinely angry. "And you're not strong yet," Jon said.

"I'm strong enough," David answered, breathing hard. Patches of scraped skin showed bright pink on his upper arms and calves.

"Hank?"

Why didn't Jon take care of the argument himself? Jon was the one who spent all that time with David, going into Boston in the evenings, playing chess, or Clue, or Parcheesi, all kinds of things Henry had deduced from what the two said to one another. Henry shrugged his shoulders and sat down on the blanket. He'd actually been afraid, like some mother with a toddler on the beach. David was more trouble than he was worth.

"I am," David said, sulky, almost whining. "I've pulled a plow."

"What?" Henry asked. Jon's mouth hung

slack, wordless. The sun poured over their backs and legs. It beat on their heads.

"Which is a lot more than either of you have done."

"What?" Henry asked again.

"Sure." David hunkered onto his heels and watched his long fingers as they rooted into the sand. Sand had matted in his hair down flat beside his face. "They commandeered all the horses, and the mules too, so Grosfader — he had a little Jewish mule to work for him."

Even Jon couldn't think of anything to say.

"I didn't know," Henry said, "that they commandeered the horses." Nobody wanted to talk, or think, about David pulling a plow, like a workhorse. And for how many planting seasons? "I didn't think anybody had a cavalry after the First World War. And the Germans were running their cars on ethyl alcohol, weren't they? Why did they take the horses?"

David looked at him, and looked at him. Food, probably, Henry thought; how stupid could you be. "I mean," he babbled into the silence, "I always figured the war was won by air power, the European front at least." Why couldn't he get off the subject of the war, and Germany, and Hitler, and by implication the death camps. Even if he disliked David there was no excuse for dragging that subject in, and why didn't Jon say something. "The Japs, on the other hand, they had a terrific air force. I don't know how they got those kamikaze pilots to do it but — "

"Henry had an uncle who was a pilot," Jon interrupted. "Shot down over Holland, right?" As if whatever Henry was saying didn't count at all. Henry let Jon take over, since Jon always thought he knew better anyway.

"Uncle William is the heroic Chapin," Jon said.

David perked up. "Chapin?"

"Henry's Boston relatives. On the maternal side, Henry's something of an American aristocrat."

"He doesn't look the part."

Jon studied Henry, too, saying nothing.

"But it's always in the blood, because appearance can be so deceptive," David said. "Blood's what they go by."

"Did you ever think of yourself as an aristocrat, Henry?"

"American aristocracy is money," Henry said.

"Ah," Jon exclaimed. "True, too true. Sad but true. Sadly true. A little money makes you better than those who have none. A lot is better than a little. Inherited fortunes rank you higher than earned income. What do you think, David, how are you going to make your first million?"

"Not by inheriting it, that's for sure," David said with a thin sound that Henry — who didn't see anything funny about it — took to be laughter.

"I'm serious." Jon shook his cousin's arm. "Have you thought about what you'll do? You'd make a good lawyer."

"And spend my life kowtowing to rich old ladies who want to leave their money to cat farms?"

"In court, dazzling a jury."

"People don't listen to me. People respond negatively to me."

"Then be a judge."

"Who'd elect me?"

"You could be appointed."

"I might as well be a Rabbi," David protested.

"Why not?" Jon asked, "Why not a Rabbi?"

"For one thing, I don't love God. Besides, I can't learn Hebrew, even the Rabbi admits it."

"There is that," Jon allowed.

A few seconds later, Jon suggested that David might like to try a career in advertising (but David hated cities) or medicine (but David couldn't stand sick people) or corporate business (but David was a Jew) or Jewish corporate business (but David couldn't even keep his pocket money straight and besides he didn't like working with people). The conversation went on until their bathing suits had dried. Henry wondered how Jon had the energy, the simple energy, to keep on suggesting possibilities for David to reject. Henry was just bored. David was too depressing.

"A parable," Jon announced. "Parable of the Undecided Farmer. There was a farmer who had one field. He plowed it and made it ready for planting, then couldn't decide what kind of seed to plant. He considered corn, wheat, grapes, tomatoes, green beans. He couldn't make up his mind what he should grow in his one field. May turned to June to July, and still he hesitated. His wife nagged at him, his neighbors scorned him. Then, one August day, he awoke to find the field grown with . . ." Jon hesitated.

"Weeds," David suggested.

"No, with grass, which became hay, which he sold to his neighbors to feed their livestock during the winter months. Because God had planted the field for him, and made the crop."

"You don't believe that," David said.

"How do I know if I believe it?" Jon pushed himself up to a sitting position. "I just now made it up, how can I tell? But I'm hungry, aren't you? How about you, Hank?"

Henry wasn't hungry, and he was going on home, but he'd see them, he said. Jon didn't say anything. David lay on his stomach and didn't move. Henry picked up his towel and walked away. Starting next week, he'd be working with Jon. Next week they'd be working in the restaurant, just him and Jon.

But while Henry worked the afternoon shift, Jon worked in the mornings. And after all, anyway, what right did Henry have to be disappointed? It wasn't as if he didn't have anything else to do with his life. He planned to get a head start on calculus over the summer, and his mother said he should read *War and Peace*; he ran three miles a day unless it was raining; he'd see Jon sometimes, he guessed, when Jon and David didn't have other plans; he had plenty to do.

On some rare occasions their days off coincided and their desires coincided, and Henry did do something with David and Jon, went out for an afternoon in the rowboat or drove up to Provincetown for an afternoon among the tourists and artists, or just spent some time on the beach. Henry thought about it, chopping mounds of parsley, mounds of dill, boning chicken breasts, filleting fish. The difference was all due to David, Henry thought, as he removed long loaves of bread from the oven and set them out on racks to cool. He couldn't kid himself about there being differences. Henry could almost hear David saying to Jon, "Have you noticed the way the guy leeches onto us?"

There was something to that, Henry had to admit, but he didn't particularly want to think about it. Because there was also, he thought, filling little bowls with softened butter and placing them in the refrigerator to chill, this question of why he felt so much of a nothing, such a nothing, so without —

What he needed, Henry thought, carrying out garbage cans, was to meet someone, some girl, maybe in the early morning when he was running and he would look at her and she would look at

114

him and they would know, almost as if they were recognizing someone they'd already met before in another life. . . . Yeah and music would play and the sun would set behind the sand dunes where they'd go to grapple. He could picture that, vividly. He could use a little grappling, never mind true love, so he could —

He was tired of being made to feel inferior, that was it, and being required to act as if that were true. He was tired of whatever it was in himself that caused things to be going on this way, and then let them just . . . go on like this. That was why, when Mr. Nafiche passed on an invitation to come early to work — "Tomorrow, my wife is making a borscht, which she tells me you have never had, and a man shouldn't die before he tastes borscht" — Henry made himself accept.

They sat around the table in the kitchen, Henry next to Jon's mother. The room smelled of baking, yeast and sugar smells; the borscht in its broad white bowl was clear as liquid rubies, with a spoonful of sour cream floating in it like a cloud in a ruby-colored sky. The Nafiches discussed apartments in Boston, because Enid wanted to move into one. This was her final year, she had to have a concert ready by next spring; besides she had a thesis to write, and the research to do; she was tired of dormitories. The Rabbi thought she was too young, Mrs. Nafiche said that if Enid thought it was necessary they wouldn't forbid her, Jon thought it would be terrific because then they could all go stay with her, and David didn't seem to care much one way or another.

Henry listened, and took slow spoonfuls of soup. He buttered and ate a thick slice of dark bread. He looked around at the brightly colored boxes and cans on the kitchen shelves, he saw Mrs. Nafiche's long golden sleeve moving in the corner of his vision, he thought he'd used to be a welcome guest at this table. Not listening to the words, he heard the tone of the conversation change and looked at Jon to hear David say, "Unless the Messiah has already come."

He had no idea how they had gotten onto the subject.

"And the Christians have him; while the Jews . . ."

The Rabbi didn't even look angry, and Mrs. Nafiche stared at her lap, and Jon looked — exhausted. Enid shifted in her chair and gathered her cardigan over her breasts and belly. Henry had no idea what was going on. He wanted to leave. He wanted never to have accepted the invitation to lunch.

"Could that be so," the Rabbi asked, "when we have been promised that we are the people of the covenant."

"The covenant," David answered without hesitation, "would seem to have been broken."

"Pah," the Rabbi said.

"Otherwise," David began, but did not finish the thought, leaving the word hanging over the table like a sword. Henry looked into his soup.

"A parable," Jon announced. David waited. "Well, a sort of parable, maybe a paradox."

"A paradigm?" Henry suggested. Jon ignored him.

"If the king has two oxen, the one strong, the other weak, which one will he choose to plow the field and bear the crops to market?"

The Rabbi's head nodded, and even Enid looked at Jon with approval.

"Lucky ox," David said.

The sound of Henry's chair legs scraping on the floor broke the hypnotic silence. "I have to go," he said.

"But you haven't finished your lunch," Mrs. Nafiche said.

"I'm sorry. It was delicious," Henry told her, although she didn't care what he thought of it. "The hot weather kills my appetite."

She nodded sympathy, Jon lifted a hand in farewell, and Henry left the room. He stopped halfway down the staircase. Angry, as if they thought they were the only people who had ever suffered, angry because they were right. He didn't know what he was getting so worked up over anyway, he told himself, it happened all the time, friends drifting apart.

Henry waylaid Jon the next time it was Jon who came down the porch steps from leaving off David for a piano lesson. "Hey, hi." He walked along beside, to see what would happen.

117

Nothing happened. "You want to swim?" Henry suggested, but Jon shook his head. When they got down to the beach, Henry suggested that they sit, and Jon complied. They sat side by side down near the waterline. Jon dug his sneakers into the sand; the two little ponds filled with water.

"Did Enid find an apartment?"

Jon nodded. Henry waited, but Jon had nothing more to say. He tried an old joke between them. "How will you stand life without her?"

"It'll be OK."

Jon stared out over the water. The one eye Henry could see, the one deep-set brown eye, looked out over nothing. Jon didn't seem to want to see Henry.

Henry, who had only wanted to be sure, stood up. He was wearing a T-shirt and shorts, but he went into the water anyway, and swam out, slowly and steadily, the taste of brine in his mouth. When he turned around to swim back in, Jon was gone.

In bed, awaiting sleep, Henry was caught up in the same old ideas, the same irresolution, the same lack of comprehension. He knew what his mother would say. She had said it often enough. "They're not like us, you've got to remember." The Marrs, the Chapins, they wouldn't just drop a friend, not the kind of friend Henry had been to Jon. (The Marrs didn't have friends, Henry reminded himself. How could you get rid of what you didn't have?) But they stuck by people, the way his mother stuck by his father and even his grandmother never actually said anything negative. Grandy didn't approve of the marriage — Chapin men were successful, Chapin women married well. That was the rule — but she'd never said anything about it.

Henry wouldn't have done this to Jon, he knew that, just shut him out like this. "C'mon, Hank," he could almost hear Jon saying it, "how can you know what you'd do?" He knew what he wouldn't do, Henry said to himself, looking at the darkness. Looking at the darkness, he remembered how the stick had felt just when it smashed into the cat's skull — and he didn't know what he might not do.

Henry just wanted things clear. If he had done this to Jon (just shut him out without a word of explanation) Jon wouldn't like it much either. Could Jon possibly think that was what Henry had done? (How could he think that; he knew Henry too well for that.) But Henry knew Jon and he thought that was what Jon had done. (But that *was* what Jon had done.) Wasn't it?

Henry didn't know. He'd tried to stay friends, despite David. Be fair, Henry said to himself, it isn't David's choice, it isn't David's fault, it's up to Jon, it's Jon's choice. The only question was, what was Henry going to do about it, and was he going to do anything.

SEVEN

Henry kept watch from the dunes, for the times when Jon and David might come up along the beach, and then waited to see if Jon might return alone. He wasn't sure why he was bothering, and every day that passed in unrewarded vigilance left him less sure that there was something to say to Jon. What did he know about friendship anyway, since Jon was the only friend he'd ever really had. Except that it was Jon, he would have ignored what was troubling him.

He would have felt better if he'd known that he could trust his own motives, and his own logic. If he could just trust himself — but Henry didn't want to think about himself, and David, and that dream that — while he had never had another like it — was the most ungovernable, ah, shit, passionate feeling he'd ever felt, even fantasizing over Enid — and except that it was Jon, Henry would have turned his back on anything to do with David.

Who now repelled him, physically — and that was genuine, the repugnance, that was about the only thing he felt sure of in his entire life. He knew David was beautiful the same way he knew the guts of a frog he was dissecting were beautiful; his mind appreciated their beauty even while his stomach wanted to vomit out everything he was seeing.

Each time the occasion eluded him Henry was relieved. Except that it was Jon.

Watching, one morning, Henry saw the two of them silhouetted against long combers that were beginning to build up whitecaps, driving across an empty ocean toward the shore. The wind whipped their trousers around their legs, and their shirts against their backs. Behind the two moving figures low gray clouds scudded across a cloudy gray sky. Henry watched their progress.

Neither Jon nor David looked up. If they had, and seen him, Henry would have waved, waved and moved on, going somewhere in the opposite direction. They rounded a curve of beach, and were out of sight. Henry sat down to wait.

Waves ran up against the shore, spread white foamy fingers and then receded, to gather for their next assault. The wind blew sand up to bite at Henry's legs and face; the wind blew his hair into his eyes. Henry wrapped his arms around his knees. The funny thing was that if it were spring this same temperature and wind would feel warm to him, and he'd be tempted to take off his clothes and go swimming, and the water would be icy cold. Since it was summer, he wanted to go home, to put on long pants and a sweater, and to stay out of reach of the water even though he knew that the warmest place to be on this kind of day was in the water.

So that if you expected something you would be sure to see it? But that would make it impossible for the truth about anything to come out; you couldn't count on yourself to know the truth. Which assumed there was a truth to be known. Which Henry was no longer so sure of. Even —

After all, he knew how he felt about this war in Korea, and Communist aggression, but he now suspected that to a native Korean it wouldn't matter very much who won or lost, which principle smashed down the other one; to a native Korean it would only matter that the fighting stop, and that daily life be allowed to go on. It might even seem that the battles had nothing to do with the individuals, and that was true, they didn't, even though it was individuals who lived or died. How could you understand it?

He saw Jon walking alone, slowly. Jon had taken off his shoes so that he could step into the waves, where the frothy water rolled up onto the sand. Jon stopped, standing ankle deep, turned, looked out over the windy water, stepped backward to sit down on the beach, buried his head between his knees, wrapped his arms over his head. Henry watched. Jon lay back full length on the sand.

Henry moved down the dune toward Jon. He was no longer sure of what he would do, say. Imagining it was different from doing it. He felt like a total jerk, but at least that was clear and simple.

With the wind gusting and waves rushing, Jon didn't hear his approach. Jon lay there, like an exhausted child who had fallen into sleep. His closed eyes left his face looking oddly unfamiliar. It was Jon's face, the big nose, the high, square cheeks, the mouth; but it was so still that Henry wasn't entirely sure he recognized it.

Henry hesitated before he crouched, gave vent to a bellow that cut into wind and waves, and leapt, landing with arms outstretched in what might have been taken for a judo stance.

Jon's eyes flew open. He gathered his body together up onto his elbows. Henry stood frozen, his silly grin plastered across his face. He didn't know what to do. He didn't know what he'd done. He thought, he'd just apologize and head away off.

"What the fuck — ?" Jon said. "Henry, by the sacred testicles of Yahweh, I don't know what you're doing. Here." Jon lay back down, closed his eyes again.

It felt as if the wind had changed direction and bowled Henry off balance. If Jon had said

Get Out of Here, just those words, in those words, it couldn't have been more clearly expressed. But — Henry sat down beside Jon, trying to clarify his own impressions — it wasn't as if Jon even cared very much whether Henry went away or not. And Jon never talked like that — not caring, using obscenity, blaspheming, that wasn't how Jon talked. That wasn't how Jon was. What had happened to him?

After a few long minutes Henry spoke carefully. "It's interesting you should say that about testicles." He kept his eyes on Jon's face. "That raises the question of the great penis in the sky. And a promise of genuine corporeality in the afterlife." There was no response. "Maybe even the possibility of unimaginable sensual pleasures — the heavenly hot dog or, if the Mohammedans are right, a gaggle of houri to . . . Well, knock on wood." Jon's eyebrows moved. "Conversely," Henry went on, "the prospect of fire, the promised roasting and toasting . . . becomes imaginable." A slow smile moved over Jon's features. Henry wasn't sure what he was waiting for, but continued. "And a theological dispute: Does God brush his teeth? If so, does He also floss?"

Jon opened his eyes, and watched Henry. As long as his eyes were open, Henry had a chance of seeing into Jon. He talked on.

"So that your latter — exclamation — might prove an unfortunate insight." Jon closed, and opened, his eyelids in assent. "The former — "

Jon watched him.

"Wait. I think I see it. I understand. You want to go out for varsity baseball next spring, and you don't want to appear immature. Listen, Jon, I can show you how to snap a wet towel. That'll help you a lot. Everybody admires a practiced towel-snapper."

Jon sat up and wrapped his arms around his knees, looking at the waves. "You're persistent, Hank. I've got to give you that."

This Henry understood. "It's my New England heritage. All that scrabbling in the earth with your bare hands to fetch out boulders so you can make fences."

Jon nodded, his face expressionless. They spoke under the noise of the wind, and waves.

Henry took a deep breath and asked, "What's going on? Jon?"

Jon turned his face and his eyes studied Henry, without humor, or even warmth. Henry swallowed and could not trust himself to say more. But he held Jon's eyes with his own, not trying to conceal how much Jon's answer mattered to him, forcing himself not to look away, and afraid.

"David," Jon said. He turned back to the water. "David isn't better. He wasn't cured, that isn't why he came to live with us. They only let him because it was the only thing they hadn't tried." Jon spoke slowly, and Henry didn't interrupt, not even to ask who *they* were. "I don't know if this cure is working. Statistically we're doing OK. But it's taking its toll of my family. And me."

Henry listened.

"The kid's suicidal," Jon announced. He turned back to Henry then. "He keeps trying to kill himself, even at the hospital under constant supervision, he'd try — starving himself or drinking stuff. He's so damnably smart — he fools you into thinking everything's fine and then you find him trying to — wrap the car around a tree, or gas himself, or — It's like having a baby around, you sense he's not in sight, you hear the silence, so you go where he's most likely to be. And he'll have taken off his shirt and be folding it up neatly on the sand, so you pretend you don't suspect, you take off your own shirt and go swimming with him. You divert him, for another day, or hour." There was expression in Jon's eyes again, now: fatigue, confusion, anxiety, anger.

"I think," Jon went on, "it's kind of like your knees. The doctors figure, if they can slow him down, make longer interludes between attempts, it'll gradually go away. In a few years. Like, the cartilage in your kneecaps is weakened every time they go out, and strengthened the longer they stay in."

Henry was nodding his head. He didn't know what to say.

"Not your problem, Henry," Jon said. "But it keeps me busy."

"It *is* my problem."

Jon shook his head.

"Because you're my friend, or you were," Henry insisted, excruciatingly embarrassed but stubbornly asking, "I miss you, Jon."

Jon's eyes comprehended. "I'm sorry, Hank. I know."

"Why didn't you tell me?"

"I wanted to. As it is written: A burden shared is a burden halved. With a friend."

Understanding how much he had misunderstood, how he hadn't lost what he had been afraid he'd lost — Henry could barely attend to Jon. He had to concentrate on what Jon was saying when what he really wanted to do was celebrate what hadn't happened.

"Besides, I figured you could help. But Ma said no, why should you be roped into problems that weren't yours. The Rabbi forbade the intrusion and Pop could argue both sides. So, the majority was against us, because Enid refused to vote."

Henry didn't need to ask why, in that case, Jon was telling him now. "Maybe we should put David onto some regimen of physical fitness — like the Army?" he suggested. "We could get him so tired he couldn't lift a knife to his throat if he wanted to." He was rewarded with a smile. "Running, biking, rowing, swimming — the trouble is, David's lazy, physically lazy. Although we could bully him into it, or you could maybe; he might agree to try it. Or am I being stupid? I mean, I really don't understand him." Henry thought and added, "I think I tend to oversimplify things."

"You've become a sadder but wiser man?" And Jon was laughing at him.

"A parable." Henry felt as if he could do anything, accomplish anything, there was such joy in him.

"That's my line."

"All right then, you do it."

"A parable," Jon said, then grinned. "OK. What was it going to be?"

"Once there was a king who had three daughters and each daughter had a harelip."

"That's sick," Jon said. "Harelips aren't hereditary," he pointed out.

Henry ignored him. "The eldest daughter hid herself away in a tower all of her life, and studied books. The second daughter allowed her father to buy her a beautiful husband. The third didn't even seem to notice her deformity. She fell in love with a shepherd who had a club foot" — Jon snorted — "and they had five children. None of the children had harelips or club feet, and they married into the middle class and lived happily ever after. However," Henry raised a hand to forestall Jon's comment, "the second daughter was plagued by jealousy — and with reason, her husband kept adding luscious morsels to his harem — until her organs of increase dried up under the constant unpleasantness and gradually she died. They buried her with full pomp and great relief. The eldest daughter . . . she wrote the definitive commentary on Aristotle's *Metaphysics*, and she has not been forgotten, even though the kingdom has long since vanished."

Jon considered what he had been told. "That's the worst parable I've ever heard."

Henry laughed aloud, into the wind. "We aim to please. But Jon, listen. Have you tried reverse psychology on David?"

"What? What is *with* you, Hank?"

"Seriously, what if you encourage him to do away with himself? According to reverse psychology, people want to do the opposite of what other people want them to do. So you give him a little pistol for his birthday — he must have a birthday, doesn't he? I bet we can think up ways to kill himself he hasn't even dreamed of. Flushing yourself down the toilet for instance. Or, eating yourself to death. Cutting off sections of your extremities like Cinderella's ugly stepsisters?"

"C'mon, Hank."

"How about the big leap? Of course, it's hard around here to find anywhere high enough to make a good job of it, but from the mast of one of those big boats, at the yacht club in Chatham — "

"Henry, you're crazy. This is absolutely nuts.

If my mother heard you — or the Rabbi — "

" — which means we'd have to figure out a way of getting out to a boat, and I'm not sure David's a strong enough swimmer. Is he?"

Jon laughed.

"No seriously." Henry dragged it out. "That's important, because what if we got him all the way out there and he was too tired to climb the mast. We'd have to haul him up and drop him, and then it would be murder."

"In more ways than one. He's not as light as he looks."

"Or, he might be so tired that his instinctive reflexes would take over, and he'd hold on."

"His instinctive reflexes are to let go." Jon was no longer laughing.

"But," Henry asked, "he clings to you."

"I never rescued anybody drowning, but you know how it's supposed to be? Henry? I'm not even sure anymore which one of us is the life-guard and which the drownee."

That, Henry thought, was the heart of it. Maybe. He let the wind blow those words around him. Was it that David wanted to destroy Jon? Because Jon hadn't been the one who was there. But David had survived, you'd think he'd be so glad and grateful just to have survived that all he'd want to do would be hang around and — be glad and grateful.

Oversimplifying again, he was doing it again. David darkened everything, confused everything, and all Henry could do was — oversimplify.

It was a long time before either of them spoke again. Henry broke the silence to ask, "What about your family? Enid sees him as another of your father's strays and that's why she's getting out?"

"There's nothing Enid can do," Jon said. "Ma — feeds him and feeds him. I think if David got fat she'd stop worrying. He outeats us all and never puts on a pound."

"What about the Rabbi?"

"The Rabbi never says, but the way he bends the rules for David — and then argues it all out, to show that bending is within the law — it's as if David is all the lost European Jewry in one body, and if he can be saved . . . I think, no I honestly do, that if David wanted to eat roast pork for a Christmas dinner, the Rabbi would find a way to justify it, and to sit down with him to the meal. And Pop just keeps trying. It's incredible, nothing gets him down for long, he's fantastic."

Henry lay back in the sand and closed his eyes. He thought more about what Jon had not said than what he'd said. Henry couldn't begin to understand David, but he knew Jon. He didn't even like David although he felt sorry for him again, so sorry it was like a physical pain — and he thought he could begin to understand what had been going on.

"He's not a kid," Henry pointed out. "He's twenty."

"Chronologically, yes. But psychologically — I don't know what he is."

Jon, too, was tired of David; it was in his voice. *That* Henry could do something about. That, he understood. He sat up and spoke briskly. "Remember Socrates and his daimon? What do you think that was?"

"How should I know?" Jon asked. "His muse? Or a spirit possessing him, what we'd call a demon? Or maybe, the voice of God. I mean, if God is now, He had to be then; so the daimon could be, like the burning bush that spoke to Moses."

"You know," Henry said, saying anything as long as it wasn't about David, "the same is true of the Greek gods. If they ever were real they still are, because they're immortal. Or the Persian, Druids, the Great Spirit. The only one that doesn't fade out is yours. The Jewish God. That's interesting, isn't it?"

"If I said that you'd accuse me of prejudice," Jon said.

"If my mother heard me saying it she'd accuse me of not enough."

"I thought she liked me."

Henry wasn't sure if Jon was mocking or what. "She does. She just — finds Jews different."

"Like the Nazis."

Henry stood up. "You can't even think that. Jon," he protested, without even thinking, and

132

then he saw the dark eyes laughing at him. Yeah, but what was so funny, he thought. He bent down and grabbed Jon's foot. He dragged Jon down toward the water. Jon writhed and protested. He had his clothes on, he said, scrabbling for handholds in the sand, he was more than a mile from home, he'd get pneumonia and it would be all Henry's fault and besides, what Henry had said wasn't true anyway, his entire basic premise was false, because of Buddha and Allah, and when he got his hands on Henry —

Jon rolled away into a sliding wave and jumped up, grabbing Henry's shoulders, pushing Henry backward into the curling top of the next wave. Henry felt his feet pulled out from under him and he relaxed, to allow the roller to revolve him upright. He was smiling to himself, and he watched Jon's victorious smirk turn to surprise when Henry tackled him around the waist and they both tumbled out into the breakers. The water, as Henry had suspected, felt warm.

EIGHT

They burst into the Marrs' kitchen, breathless from the run up the beach into the wind, but no longer dripping water. Both of Henry's parents were in the kitchen and David was with them. Mrs. Marr waited by the stove for the kettle to boil; Mr. Marr and David waited at the table. "What happened to you two?" Henry's mother asked.

Henry looked at Jon, and Jon looked at Henry, and they just grinned. "I'm going to change," Henry said. "You want to borrow some clothes?"

"Just a sweater maybe, I'm OK."

"What did you do, fall in the water?" Mrs. Marr asked.

"You might say that," Jon told her. "Yeah, let's say that."

Henry ran up to his room, to change quickly

into dry clothes from the skin out, to pick out his baggiest sweater for Jon, to hurry back downstairs. They'd be all right, he and Jon; together they could deal with David. He already had an idea and he asked his mother about it while he set out mugs for her, and a box of cookies. "We don't have any lemon," his mother apologized, "but there's milk. And sugar."

"Mom, would it be all right if — if the weather's OK — if we had a picnic supper on the beach tomorrow night? David, do you want to?"

He'd succeeded in surprising David.

"Just hot dogs and potato chips, nothing fancy. You know the kind of thing. A fire. Lukewarm sodas."

"You make it sound so exciting," David said.

"Then I'm lying. It's not exciting at all, is it, Jon?"

"Boring. Ostensive definition of boring," Jon agreed. "I'd enjoy it, Hank. How about you, David?"

David glanced uneasily at Henry's father. "I don't know."

"It was only a suggestion," Mr. Marr said.

Henry's mother poured hot water into the mugs, then sat down with them and passed around the box of tea bags. "If you decide you don't want the ticket, David, I'll use it, so it won't go to waste. Edwin would enjoy your company, you might enjoy the concert, that's what we thought."

"We can picnic anytime," Henry said.

"Yes, but I've never picnicked. It would be like being a *Saturday Evening Post* cover. I've always wanted to live in two dimensions. But, I don't want to seem ungrateful, Edwin."

"I wouldn't be disappointed," Henry's father said.

"Do I have to make up my mind right away? It's not until tomorrow."

"There's no rush," Henry assured him. "It all depends on the weather anyway — if this is new weather blowing in or if it's going to settle down and rain for days."

"Is it raining?" his mother asked.

"It was starting to."

"Then I'd better drive you two home," she told Jon.

"Thank you," David said, "but I'd rather walk."

Henry's mother looked at David for a minute, then she looked at Jon, then she said, "You can walk if you want to. Jon's already been thoroughly soaked so I'm driving *him*. You have no choice, Jon."

"If I have no choice," Jon said. "then you don't either, David. So much for free will. You'll tell us when it's a good time for you, won't you, Mrs. Marr?"

"When we've finished our tea is the best time for me," she said.

In the empty kitchen, Henry washed the empty mugs and his father lingered at the table. The rain fell heavily outside the door, a sudden summer rain. "Probably he'll go to the concert," Henry said.

"Would *you*?"

How could he answer that since he'd never been asked.

"For David," his father said, "the important thing is to have a choice. Then he can decide what he wants to do. So he can do the opposite."

"That's crazy." Henry didn't know how much his parents knew about David, or understood; they never asked why he was always accompanied to his lessons, and home again after. But they didn't ask questions about anything, or anybody.

"Destructive, more," his father said. "Or self-punishing? I imagine the Nafiches also must be wondering how immutably the past shapes us. One's own past, and choices, too. I admire your friend's family," his father said.

Henry didn't know what to respond, so he nodded his head.

"But I don't envy them David." Mr. Marr got up to bring Henry his mug. "Although you're right, I do. How could I not?"

Henry couldn't answer that.

He worked it out: The object was to save David, or rescue him — from himself, or from his death. Or from death itself, if Henry wanted to get poetic about it. He could almost picture it. He and Jon on one side, and the dark thing on the other, and David in the middle, like a human rope in a tug of war. The Nafiches also were on their side, and his father. Odd, that he didn't know about his mother. Odd, too, that David himself, both as battlefield and as prize, should seem so weak to him, and helpless.

He thought it out as he sat on the beach waiting for David and Jon. Because David hadn't shown up by four and the sky had cleared at midday, his parents had gone off to Boston together. They wouldn't be back until midnight. Henry took his time over preparations, packing a paper bag of food and utensils, gathering wood for a fire and piling it up on the sand, peeling the bark off of three long green branches and setting them upright in the sand. Warm, clear, and windless, it was a perfect evening. He actually hated beach picnics, with sand getting into everything, but he planned this one to be as good as he could make it. He waited on the beach, watching the gilded water recede from the shore into a low tide, content. He and Jon together — as long as they were working together, David didn't have a chance.

David and Jon walked up along the shore; each carried a six-pack of beer, not even in a bag. "We didn't want to come empty-handed to your little party," David told him.

"But how did you?" Henry asked Jon.

"David did it."

"Do you have a fake ID?

"They don't care who they sell liquor to, as

long as they're not caught. Jon and I just went down to Hyannis where nobody knows us. The guy figured we were tourists, so he didn't care."

"Do you think that was why?" Jon asked his cousin. "I thought it was because you were so mature-looking, and then you got huffy at the right time."

"Jon," David explained to Henry, "looks Jewish, so he couldn't be local, right? I, on the other hand, look like someone up from Connecticut, or Westchester County. I just told him I'd left my driver's license in my wallet, which was back at the hotel, and he wanted to believe me. It's no big deal. He doesn't care about us as long as we're not local so we can't get him into trouble."

They set the bottles in the shade behind a dune and swam in mild, waveless water. Henry stayed in the water while David and Jon sat on a blanket and drank beer from bottles. The sun lowered, a little breeze rose up, and the temperature dropped.

Henry started the fire and sat down to drink with them while they waited for the flames to make coals. The beer tasted good, which was a pleasant surprise. It went with the hot day, and his sun-dried salty skin, it suited the sense of stretching out on the beach to watch darkness roll in over the water, a sense of well-being, and his own strength, and plenty of time to get everything he wanted from his life. "Is this the kind of thing you do in Boston?" he asked, looking over to Jon's profile, beyond David's reclining form.

"There are no beaches in Boston, Henry. You've studied geography, you know that."

"I mean sit and drink and talk. You knew what I meant."

"It's part of what we do," David said. "Why?"

"Just curious."

"After which we move on to the more interesting activities. Don't we?" David asked.

Jon didn't say anything. David wanted Henry to ask, What more interesting activities? so Henry did. "David," Jon protested, warned.

"You mean you haven't told him?"

"Told me what?"

"I thought you two were such friends."

Henry turned to look at Jon.

"We pick up girls," Jon said. "Well, women. You know Hank." David leaned back on his elbows, enjoying Henry's reaction. Jon didn't want to talk about it; Henry could see that. David wanted to make him talk about it.

"I'm hungry," Henry said. "I've got some branches here — are you two ready? I'm going to eat now, do either of you want to join me?"

"You don't like me, do you?" David asked him.

Henry, already going to fetch the branches, turned around slowly and stared down at David's handsome face. He considered possible responses. "Why?" he finally asked. "Do you want me to?"

That must have been the right one because David relaxed. He turned his face to the horizon, where lightlessness was being translated into darkness. Henry looked to Jon, to know if he should say something else, say more to David.

"Are the hot dogs kosher, that's what I want to know," Jon said.

"Jon, I never thought — "

"I was kidding. Anything cooked outside over an open fire is automatically OK. I'm sure of it."

Henry looked up from the stick he was threading a hot dog onto. "That can't be true, is that true?"

"Except shellfish, but they're not roasted, they're steamed anyway. Over here, David — you're about to be initiated into an ancient rite."

They roasted the hot dogs, put them into rolls, spread mustard with their fingers, and ate. Henry passed around the bag of potato chips. David passed around bottles of beer. Night spread over the sky and water. It was as if the three of them were on an island of flickering light and flickering warmth, the only island in the whole dark sea. They fed the fire and drew the blankets in close to it. David drank steadily, apparently unaffected; Henry felt the beer thicken his tongue and set the bottle down, aside. He couldn't tell about Jon, if he was drinking, if it was having any effect on him. A few stars appeared. The fire burned down to coals.

Jon's voice spoke out of the flickering shadows across the fire. "Sometimes I think about the Indians that used to live around here. Do you know anything about them, Henry? It must have been a hard life, in order to survive you'd have to fish and hunt and farm, too, all three."

"All I know about them is that they welcomed the Pilgrims — "

"Or so the story goes," Jon said. "But that's a story the Pilgrims told, we don't know how the Indian version goes."

"I can't even remember the name of the tribe. Can you?"

"Was it one of those tribes that buries its dead aboveground?" David asked.

"That's a contradiction in terms," Jon pointed out.

"You're deliberately misunderstanding me," David said. "Don't play dumb with me, Jon."

"OK," Jon agreed happily.

"In some places out West, the Indian burial grounds were full of platforms, and the dead man lay on the platform — in full regalia, according to what I read. I'd like to see one of those burial grounds, the dead set out for wind and weather to do their work."

"Why?" Henry asked. If Jon thought the topic was all right, and he must since he hadn't changed it, and since David had brought it up, he might as well try to find out what David was thinking. Most of his information about David, after all, was hearsay.

"Everybody carries on so about the pyramids," David said, as if that explained anything.

"Do you mean the way they used to hide the dead bodies away underground, under tons of stone, all eviscerated and embalmed and wrapped up for eternal life?"

"Nicely phrased, Henry. I didn't know you were a connoisseur of irony."

Henry didn't know if that was a compliment.

"Dust to dust, as it is written," Jon said. "The Indians and the Egyptians, both have it wrong. I think, I'd like to be buried with an acorn in my navel, to make an oak tree."

Henry, who would have preferred burial at sea except for that moment when the body slips from beneath the covering and — white shrouded — enters the water, raised the possibility of cremation. Probably, he thought, as he spoke, you had to balance on a narrow line with someone like David, between talking about it all the time and never mentioning it at all, because if you never mentioned it then it gained in power, like any taboo subject. Besides, he was interested in what Jon had to say, and in what he himself had to say. "The idea of rotting" — he looked at Jon's face, at David's — "it's — pretty repulsive."

"Even the sinews of the Chapins must come to it," Jon reminded him. "Although, the way they do autopsies — a good Christian must begin to wonder what the Day of Judgment will look like. I mean, you can't tell me those doctors do more than a quick basting stitch when they're through, and who knows how they put the organs away, all helter-skelter and not at all to the eternal plan. What God will think. . . ."

"Like I said, cremation," Henry repeated, the vision all too clear before him.

"Jews can't," Jon told him.

"Really?"

"Against the law. So it's me for earth, with a seed in my navel. Which do you think is the real me, Hank? A fruit tree or a hardwood?"

"One of those Japanese trees, what are they called? Those tiny little trees with adorable miniature branches, you know?"

Jon leapt up in answer and tackled him, not as roughly as it might have looked. They wrestled across the sand.

"You can't say that."

"But I did, so I clearly can."

"Then take it back."

"You can't take words back, Jon, be reasonable."

Henry was laughing so hard he could barely defend himself.

Until David's voice cut across their grunts and laughter — "Some Jews did" — thin and cold even on the warm night, even across the hot coals.

"Whole towns," David continued, "stank for years from the smoke of the crematoria," as if they had asked him what he meant. "Good, clean little German towns, ruined — so Grosfader told me — and the people couldn't take their morning coffee outdoors on balconies the way they liked, because of that smell."

Henry looked at Jon, who shook his head briefly. Meaning what? David stared into the fire. Henry, not really part of this, drew back and waited for Jon to give the lead. David opened another bottle of beer, drank deep, and loosed his voice on them.

"Grosfader kept Ulli informed, like a bedtime story, how many Jews expunged, how many cities now cleansed of the contagion, how many the ovens could handle, in an hour, a day, a week. Ulli had been circumcised. It would be useless to run away. Some Jews did not circumcise their sons — hoping to save them." David spoke without emotion. "There was of course no hope. No way. Only one way. The dressing rooms first, and you took off everything, even your wedding ring; then naked together into the big rooms. Bodies like worms in a basket. The ovens. If it hadn't been for the gold fillings and teeth, it would have been easy from then on. But somebody had to find the gold. Don't you wonder, Jon? I do, who waded through those ashes, raked through the bones and teeth, to find gold. Some kid, bent on survival." David stared into the fire, where coals glowed vermillion and cooled to gray.

"A boy, probably. The girls were used for

whores, if they were pretty; and the women, if they weren't too old. They were numbered and taken away, although some of them were used for experimental purposes. The others, not pretty, not of useful age — simple economics. The cost of Kotex pads, for example — this was money that needed to be put into munitions, matériels better used for bandages. Those who died right away were probably the lucky ones, don't you think?" He looked across the fire at them.

Henry stared back at David's face, waiting for Jon to say something. By now, everybody knew atrocities had been committed, but David knew precisely what they were; and he knew the victims, precisely who they were. So did the Nafiches.

Jon said, his voice heavy and thick as if his throat like Henry's had closed off, "Some got out. Some were hidden."

"Grosfader told me," David's thin voice said, "what happened if you were caught harboring a Jew. This is something you can identify with, Henry. They knew how to peel a man's skin away — rather like the way you skin chicken breasts for Uncle Leo I'd imagine — " Henry gathered his knees up against his stomach. Trying not to hear, but the sharp voice cut through all the deafness he put up against it. "My mother was not like yours," David told Jon. "She wasn't at all pretty," he said, as if someone had accused her of it.

Henry was curled up now around his stomach, and he wanted them both to go away. Stars hung over them. The water sucked at the shore.

"It's a lucky thing for Ulli that he wasn't Jewish. Grosfader said, even the little children, all of them sent naked into the big rooms. When Mutti went away to get married, she had to go away to get married, he said I should stay at home with him. She died in Berlin, or someplace else, in an air raid — Grosfader told me and I cried, but I think he told terrible lies sometimes. There were no more letters after that, and just Grosfader and Ulli left. They were lucky, Grosfader said; they had food to eat." He stopped. Henry held his breath, hoping it was over.

"They killed all the best men," David said, in a new voice, analytical. Henry felt as if David was pointing the voice at him now. Why didn't Jon say something, do something? "Only the dregs were left at the end. Survived. There is no satisfaction in surviving. You have to admit that."

"You weren't even in the camps," Jon said in that slow, thick voice.

"Yes," David agreed, "but I should have been."

An empty silence, hollow, held them — for a long time — a silence the breeze did not penetrate, nor the waves, nor the light from the dying fire. Finally, "Let's go," Jon's voice said. Henry didn't look up from the darkness of his knees. He felt Jon's hand on his shoulder, just for a second. He knew the hand was warm, but he felt no warmth. He heard the two of them walking away through sand, David and Jon, walking away.

David came here, dragging horrors behind him like a bride's train. No wonder he didn't look behind him. Henry could understand why David wanted to die. Henry had never felt such fear before, fear of everyone else in the world, and fear of himself, and fear for himself. What he might do, what they might do. There was nothing they might not do.

He stood up. He picked up the beer bottles and put them in the paper bag, threw handfuls of sand on the embers, and his hands shook. In battle, at least, you were fighting, with men fighting beside you.

The water moved up against the shore. The black night closed over him. Poised at the water's edge, Henry listened, and thought: Because he didn't understand how they could have stood having it happen to them. Or how anyone could do that, to women and children, too. It was easier to imagine doing it than enduring it —

Which was worse. Because it meant what he was like. And he knew he was more like most people than Jon was. What he was really like, and what most people were really like —

And they went just like cattle to be slaughtered, they just climbed onto the boxcars and let it be done to them. You couldn't respect them very —

Henry wrapped his hands around his ears and over his face.

Eventually, Henry made his way home, carrying the debris of the evening. He didn't think he would be able to fall asleep, but he did, and awoke to the question: Why did the Nafiches want so badly to save David when so many had been lost. What was the use?

NINE

He wasn't hungry, he couldn't concentrate on *War and Peace*, he didn't have the will to run — if either of his parents had tried to speak to him he couldn't have answered. He went outside, and down to the beach, and walked. Away from town, away from everyone, away. He couldn't find — the ice to skate on over the black vortices David had shown him; he couldn't even find a word for them. He didn't want to think, he didn't want to know, he didn't want to understand.

He stood, finally, entirely still at the edge of the waves' reach, trying to feel himself into the heavy rhythms of the water, away from the human world. Jon found him there and went straight to the point. "I'm sorry, Hank, I didn't know he was going to do that. He'd never talk about it before, not to anyone, not even at the hospital."

"Where is he?"

"Working with Pop, I begged off. Henry? I really am sorry."

Henry kept his eyes on the surface of the water. Jon had known all along, and had kept the secret. Henry ought to feel grateful but he didn't. He felt betrayed.

"It doesn't matter."

"It's because he hates you," Jon said. The waves nibbled at their bare feet. "Because you're not Jewish, so you don't have the burden."

Henry didn't bother with disguise. "That's shit."

"Look, I didn't *want* you to hear all that. I was going to come back, but he wouldn't go to bed. Henry, are you angry at *me*?"

"You knew," Henry explained. "You knew all along." He felt Jon looking at him, standing beside him. "You always knew."

"Sit down," Jon ordered. "What is it? The atrocities — horror? But what did you think, Henry? What did you think had gone on? Or is it that I — we — enjoy our lives, my family, me. I said, sit." Henry obeyed.

Maybe Jon didn't understand. Maybe, being Jon, he couldn't imagine.

"What? Henry?" Jon sat beside him.

Henry watched the water, floating, and declined to answer. "I don't know." Jon could have forewarned him, and he should have — not about David, David wasn't Jon's fault, but about — "It doesn't matter."

Beside him Jon sat silent. For a long time. The ridged gray water rolled up, one wave upon another, surged onto the sand. Each wave, breaking, separated itself from the one before. Finally, Henry turned his head to look at Jon. The breeze blew Jon's hair around, and blew his tears so that his cheeks were wet as if he had been swimming.

What was the matter with Jon? Henry was embarrassed, and worried, in succession and then simultaneously. What should he do? Jon didn't seem to notice. But they were too old to cry, he was too old.

"Why should he have to go on living with it?" Henry asked, trying to explain even though he knew Jon would never understand the explanation. "Or any of us."

"As it is written," Jon answered, without looking at Henry, without wiping his eyes. "*See, I have set before thee this day life and good, and death and evil.*" Then he did look straight at Henry, and continued, "*I call heaven and earth to record this day against you, that I have set before you life and death, blessing and cursing: Therefore choose life, that both thou and thy seed may live.*"

That was Jon's answer. It was Jon's kind of answer, and it wasn't good enough.

"But, Jon, the Jews — they didn't choose — or if they did, it didn't make any difference.

And David didn't. None of us do. We just suffer, endure, and alone."

"Not alone, Hank. That's the mistake. I mean, we're friends." Jon wiped at his eyes. "For better or worse, richer or poorer, in sickness and in health."

"You can't turn everything into a joke. Or anyway, I can't."

"Hank, listen." Jon's voice was urgent. "Pop told me, years ago, when I began to know what had happened to us. What had been done. The death camps. Hank, I never forget, and every time I remember . . ."

Henry hadn't thought. Jon wouldn't forget; Henry knew that.

"Pop said, when he was in the trenches — and he was there, he's been there, and the trenches were . . . bad, Henry, you know that. Pop said a lot of the men were just waiting to die. And get it over with. They knew what the odds were, and they just waited there, scared and waiting, hoping it would be quick. Just sitting. No conversations. Everybody alone. Pop said, you do have to choose, and he refused to side up with death. If you choose life, I think — Hank, are you listening?"

"I'm listening." He was, he was listening to Jon's words, and his voice, and to the expressions on his friend's face, listening to his speaking eyes. He was listening to the succession of words but only as a single instrument in an orchestrated piece.

"Then you're choosing all the — terrible — things, the worst you can imagine and you've got the imagination, Hank, don't kid yourself. But that's only part of it. You're also choosing to celebrate."

"Yeah, but what if you're wrong?"

Jon laughed aloud. "Right, wrong — what difference is that going to make?" The sound of his laughter washed over Henry like waves, immersing him temporarily in Jon's freedom.

Henry understood. He almost choked, as if the water were actual. He'd had it all wrong. He'd thought that it was he and Jon on one side, with David in the middle; but it was Jon in the middle, Jon David wanted to destroy, or needed to defeat, or whatever it was that drove David. Jon had no idea. But the game — and it wasn't a game — was being played between Henry and David.

Jon was looking at Henry, waiting for an answer, but Henry couldn't say anything. He didn't know if he was any match for David. In fact, he was pretty sure he wasn't.

"So," Jon asked him, "are you going to stick it out with me?"

"I don't know if I've got the strength."

"You do," Jon told him. "Whether you want to or not, I'm afraid you do."

Henry shook his head, doubting.

"Where's the Chapin spirit?" Jon demanded, standing up. "Never-say-die, pride and rectitude, endurance, good old New England greed — the spirit that founded the nation."

Henry took a deep reluctant breath and stood up with Jon. Nothing had changed, except he had seen what David was up to. Henry didn't care if David was one hundred percent right about everything, he wasn't going to just let the guy destroy Jon. Not and just stand there. This was between him and David. He understood that now. He'd been such a jerk, such an innocent, he hadn't understood that before. "OK," Henry said.

They clambered up the sides of the dunes and slid down them, taking the more arduous way because it was the longer way. "OK," Henry said again, "but what am I supposed to do?"

He was listening to Jon and to his own thoughts simultaneously. Jon only had his hands on half of what was going on and that was the way Henry wanted it to stay. But Henry had to know more.

"What you do is just tell him the truth. Whatever that is, at any given moment, that's all you can do. He knows when he's being lied to."

"Do *you* do that?"

"How can I?"

That was what Henry suspected; and he suspected that David knew it, too.

"I think," Jon said, "it's maybe because we're Jews so we have to lie, as he sees it. But you're not, so you can't. Because he'll believe what you say. If you lie to him, it's because he's a Jew, and he can see through to whatever you're lying about. Because he'll never trust you."

"Then why should he believe me?"

"He has to, because he doesn't trust you, because you're not a Jew so you don't have to lie."

"That's crazy, Jon. It's also pretty stupid." Half of Henry's mind was busy considering how much of what Jon perceived about David was what David wanted him to perceive, and why that might be what David wanted his cousin to think; the other part was busy considering where the real truth might lie, because Henry's battle was going to be where the real truth was, not where David wanted Jon to think it was.

"Crazy's what it's about," Jon said. "Nobody said he wasn't crazy. It's cured, he isn't. On the other hand — look at the bright side — he isn't dead yet either."

"Jon, what if I just wasn't around?" If David thought he'd won, would he lay off? That was the question.

"No," Jon said quickly. "He needs you."

"Needs me? What for?" David wouldn't be so stupid; and besides, just getting rid of Henry wouldn't answer what David wanted, that was only a prelude to what David wanted, some necessary prelude, maybe. Henry hoped it was necessary.

Jon had started laughing again. "He needs you there to hate and envy and despise — "

Henry was laughing, too.

" — but it's true, Hank. They also serve, remember. The doctors said, my parents asked the doctors. You give him something to think about, trying to figure you out."

Because Jon was vulnerable through Henry. David would use that. He'd used it last night, that was the real weapon he'd used, and Jon, not Henry, was his real target.

"Besides," Jon said, "you have to think of me. You're my best audience. You wouldn't deprive me of that, would you?"

Not if he could help it he wouldn't. "That's pretty arrogant," he pointed out.

"I'm sorry," Jon said.

"No you're not," Henry told him.

"You're right, I'm not. But I probably should be, don't you think?"

TEN

It didn't take David long to figure out what Henry was up to. Jon, being Jon, never thought of it, which was all Henry asked for.

The long July days went by and whenever he could Henry interposed himself. If they were walking, he placed himself between David and Jon. He often asked Jon to allow him to work mornings as well as afternoons "for the money." He suggested outings when they had the same days off — to the famous rock at Plymouth, to Salem. During those long drives he sat in the backseat but leaned forward, his elbows spread out between the two in the front.

The Plymouth hegira, as David called it, went without hitch. The Salem pilgrimage failed, from David's first sight of the great-rooted chestnut trees lining the streets, and the big square houses set out on their green lawns like pearls that knew well their own price.

David parked the car and they stepped out of it into a sun-stained day. They meandered down the sidewalk, admiring the polished door knockers. "This is your natural habitat, Henry, isn't it?" David asked.

"Not exactly." Henry refused to rise to that bait. "You've been in my house, David."

"This is more like the paradise lost," Jon suggested. "What a day, isn't it? I don't think I'd like to live here, but it sure is pretty. Did any Chapins ever live in Salem? Is there a Chapin house we can look at? You can tell us, Hank, we won't be impressed."

"They hanged the Salem witches." David's tone was conversational. "I wonder what they did with the bodies, I can't imagine they gave them burial, maybe they burned them after. Do you know?"

Jon stopped, and looked around him. Henry felt like kicking David but then, looking at the blank, handsome face he felt like weeping, and finally, looking up and down the street, with its damned unconcerned richness, its plump security —

"Let's get out of here," Jon said.

Henry almost never saw Jon alone, and then not for more than a few minutes. One of those brief times he asked his friend what it was like "with a whore."

Jon turned red under his tan, shook his head, and wouldn't say anything.

"OK," Henry said. "I can't make you, and I won't ask again, but I want you to know, I'll be wondering. I just want you to know that. I'm wondering right now."

"Lay off, Hank," Jon said. But Henry meant it as a joke.

Sundays, the restaurant didn't open until one. Sunday mornings, especially sunny Sunday mornings, were luxuriously lazy times for the Nafiches. Often Mrs. Nafiche came outside to sit with her family wearing what she called only her bathrobe but it looked to Henry like something a movie star might wear, to be photographed at home in. Not Marilyn Monroe but someone foreign, Ingrid Bergman maybe. Henry would have called it a gown, a flowing purple gown that made a sound like the rushing of waves. On the first Sunday in August, he came early to work and met Mrs. Nafiche going inside to change. She greeted him gladly then turned for a final glimpse of the three young people seated around the table at the end of the lawn. David stood up. He planted his feet apart to raise binoculars to his eyes and scan along the width of the harbor, where little green rental boats bobbed.

"He is beautiful, isn't he?" Mrs. Nafiche said. "I think sometimes I'd like to have a statue made of him. Perhaps in marble, there's a Ligurian marble that . . . Tell me," she smiled at Henry with moist eyes, "I know, I'm a foolish old woman."

"Not old," Henry said.

"You, you're catching all of Jon's bad habits." She rested her hand on his shoulder, briefly, before turning away. Henry joined Jon, and David, and Enid at the table. He sat down between David and Jon.

"Do they ever catch anything in the harbor?" he asked. "Has anyone ever seen any of them catching anything?"

Nobody answered. He didn't expect an answer. Jon had pulled his chair back, out of the shade of the umbrella, and sat stretched out to the sun, his eyes closed. David sat down, still holding the binoculars to his eyes.

"David?" Henry asked. "Are the fledglings still in the nest?" Straining to make sense of the dark mass that was all he could distinguish at the distance, in the bright light, his vision was confused.

David answered without moving. "Of course. It's not until about forty-eight to fifty-seven days after hatching that they can fly."

"I remember when there would be lots of ospreys," Enid said. "When we first moved up here, you're too young to remember it, Jon, there were ospreys all around."

"Ospreys are hawks," David said.

"Probably," Jon spoke lazily, without opening his eyes, "all the people around drive them away. Soon it'll be like the dodo bird, and we'll say to our grandchildren — just like cave grandparents must have said to their cave grandchildren 'Why, I remember the dodo.' Why, I remember the osprey."

"You mean they're becoming extinct?" Henry asked. "Like the buffalo?"

"Like the Jews," David said.

"The Jews," Henry pointed out to David's profile, "are hardly extinct. Ask the Arabs."

"*You* ask the Arabs," Jon peered at him from a half-open eye. "I have a previous engagement."

"What is that boat doing?" A rowboat had approached the second marker and seemed to be staying there. Henry pointed. The adult osprey rose up out of the nest.

"Looks like they're tying up," David told him.

Enid shaded her eyes, to see more clearly. "That's why the osprey are disappearing."

Jon reached across Henry to take the binoculars. The osprey looped and dipped through the air, circling her nest. Henry could hear her faint, whistling, wheepling cries of alarm.

"Let me see," David asked. Jon passed the glasses across. "Look at that," David said, and gave the glasses to Henry.

Henry wasn't sure at first what he was seeing. A narrow, dark head, beaked, held stiffly above water. The wings hunching up through waves like some clumsy butterfly stroke, like the butterfly stroke if the swimmer's arms had been amputated. Henry didn't want to know what he was seeing.

He wondered what the boat tied up to the marker was going to do. Two men, and a boy, sat in it, all with their backs turned to the fallen fledgling, all ignoring the frantic osprey above, all apparently eating. Sandwiches, Henry thought.

He swept the harbor with the glasses — some of the people in some of the other boats had their faces turned toward the event.

"Where's it heading?" Jon asked. David took the binoculars from Henry.

"Aren't they going to do something?" Henry asked.

"Heading toward shore," David reported. "Is there anywhere where it can climb up?"

"Not unless he goes beyond the seawall." Henry's eyes were on the tiny black head, the dark distant struggling shape. "Are any of those boats moving?" Henry asked Jon. "Can you see?"

"If I don't get some practicing done," Enid said, and stood up.

"Could we get out there in time?" Jon asked Henry. "Do you think?"

"There's nothing you can do," David said.

"If we did, what could we do?" Henry asked.

"I don't know. Something, maybe. Hank?"

"You can't do anything," David said. "You

don't know what to do, how to handle wild animals." He held the binoculars steady at his eyes, watching. "It's getting tired, anyway. Its feathers must be sodden, those immature feathers soak up water much more quickly, much more completely, too."

Neither Jon nor Henry paid any attention. David accompanied them down to the rowboat and uncleated the line for them. They settled themselves onto the rowing seat. As they pulled away from the stone wall, each on an oar, David returned to the table, the binoculars at his eyes.

Henry followed the pace Jon set at the oars. Every now and then he turned his head to check their direction, and their progress. "Head's not up so high," he reported.

"Sail on," Jon urged him. Their four feet were braced in a line against the stern seat. "Sail on and on. At least the waves aren't bad, that's something."

"Bad enough for the bird," Henry said. The boat moved steadily.

"As it is written," Jon grunted. "Sufficient unto the day — are the waves thereof. We'll get there."

"Then what?"

"How should I know? We'll think of something. It should be too weak," he took a grunting breath, "to do us much harm."

The harbor was hundreds of yards across. The shore drew steadily away from them, and David diminished. Henry looked over his shoulder, reset his hands on the oar, and asked, "Can you pull any faster?"

"I can if you can."

Sweat ran down their faces, down their backs, down under their armpits.

"Wait. Just — a — minute," Jon gasped. "Out of — shape — breath — "

They were catching up with the bird, which hunched slowly away from them, heading toward the flat harbor wall. Narrow shoulders lifted up; waves flowed by the bird's eyes. While they watched, water-weighted wings lifted, fell and the head sank beneath a rise of water that hurried on to cradle their boat. The osprey fluttered overhead, wheepling.

"Is it alive?" Henry asked. "It moved. Did it move?"

"No," Jon said.

Little waves slapped the sides of the boat. The osprey moved overhead, in the corner of their vision. The place where the fledgling had been was empty now.

"Hey, kid?" a man's voice called. They looked around to locate it: One of the men in the rowboat, still tied up to the marker, the boat bobbling at the end of its short securing line.

"I'm real sorry, kid," the man called through cupped hands. "We lost our anchor. We had to tie up someplace. To eat." He held up a half-eaten sandwich in explanation. He waited a minute, and then added, "Anyway, I'm sorry." He turned back to his companions and his lunch.

Jon picked up the oar, without a word. Henry followed his lead, without a word. They rowed back across the harbor.

David greeted them. "Hail the conquering heroes." He took the bow line and wound it around the big iron cleat, then stood back to give them room to climb up, first Jon, to whom Henry passed up the oars, then Henry, who took the oars from his friend.

At least they tried, at least they didn't just sit back and watch things go wrong. But trying didn't matter much, unless you at least succeeded; to the bird anyway. It was no consolation to Henry to know he'd tried to do the right thing. He suspected it was no consolation to Jon either.

"Feel better, Jon?" David asked his cousin.

"The human race," Jon said, almost humorously, "hasn't come along as far as it might have."

"It never will," David promised him. "Except for you, of course. Oh, and Henry, too, of course, except for the two of you."

"Will you just shut the hell up?" Henry demanded. He could take the oars, both of them, holding them by the handles and swinging wide — and smash them into David's perfect face, and lay open his cheek. He could imagine how that would happen, and how it would look, and how it would feel to do that. He wanted to mark David's face with blood, with bones and teeth, with pain.

David smiled at him, in perfect understanding.

ELEVEN

Henry had what he took to be a brilliant idea. "A musical evening," he said, sitting up. "Like something out of Tolstoy."

Neither Jon nor David paid any attention to him. David lay on his stomach, watching his fingers make shallow tracks in the sand. Jon lay on his back with his eyes closed, letting an early August sun pour down on his chest.

"Listen, aren't you even going to listen?"

"What are you thinking of, a going-away party?" David asked.

"We only stay at my grandmother's a week," Henry told him. "It hardly merits celebration. No — I was thinking if, everybody sort of did something, some performance kind of thing. Jon? What do you think?"

Jon sat up and studied the back of David's

head. It would be a project, Henry thought; preparation for the occasion would keep David occupied for a few days.

"You mean, the people who are musical can do musical things? Like Enid and your father. David could play piano — "

"Not in mixed company." David rolled around to sit facing them.

His father had said what David wanted to do was what he wouldn't do. Henry's suspicion was that David did what he thought you didn't want him to do, or didn't do what you let him know you wanted him to. "Aren't you any good?" Henry asked.

"You should know by now, I'm good at everything I do."

"So you'll play?" Henry couldn't say what he was thinking. That David didn't seem to be very good at killing himself.

"I might."

"Ma can sing," Jon offered, "but what about your mother?"

"She could probably recite something. She's got plenty of poems memorized. Will the Rabbi come?"

"We'd have it at our house," Jon said, "so he might. He could read us a psalm in Hebrew. Have you ever heard Hebrew, Hank?"

Jon knew he hadn't.

"A lot will depend on who asks who to do what," Jon said.

"Whom," Henry said.

"Who asks who to do whom."

"C'mon, Jon."

"Whom asks who? The king asked the queen and the queen asked — "

"Jon," Henry realized, "what about me? What can I do? I can't do anything."

"There is that," David said.

"We'll help you think of something, won't we, David?"

"Sure. Glad to."

Henry could imagine what David would cook up for him.

"Listen, Hank. I've got an idea. You know that poem we did this year, 'A poem should be palpable and mute,' remember? You could write out copies of it and hand them around to everyone and then stand there — palpable and mute, don't you see? What do you think?"

Henry pictured it, all of them sitting around the Nafiches' table, himself in suit and tie standing silent in front of them while they all read silently. . . . "That's funny," he said. "I won't do it, but it's pretty funny."

"We should have a program," David volunteered.

"What do you mean a program?" Jon asked.

"A list of who's going to do what, in the order of appearance. I know something about lettering, I took calligraphy in Connecticut. Therapeutic calligraphy."

"Sounds good," Jon said, "but we shouldn't

put down what people will do. Just the names. How good are you, David, seriously?"

"Very good," David assured him. "Seriously good. But why can't I say what the person is going to perform?"

"In case anyone wants to surprise us. Maybe Henry, for example, would like to surprise us."

"You're just trying to make me feel more inadequate than I already do."

"Would we do that?" David asked.

"Yes," Henry answered, louder than he'd meant.

"A parable," Jon announced. He was sitting cross-legged on his towel. "The Parable of the Dinner Party. Once there was a master who had four servants. He gave a banquet, to which he invited the most important men of the town, the mayor, the tax collector, the priest, the doctor, the chief of police. They all accepted. He called his servants before him and ordered each one of them to provide some entertainment, during the course of the courses. The first servant, who danced as gracefully as a girl, said that he would dance. The second, who sang with a voice like the nightingale, would sing. The third, whose skill on the flute was such that he could make music that rippled like the little waters, would play the flute. The fourth, who danced like the turtle, who sang like the peacock, whose breath on the pipes made noises like mourning frogs, did not know what to do. When the day came, he stood before the banquet table and did nothing. The guests found this humorous so the master's anger was ameliorated. After a while, the fourth servant's memory of humiliation faded and he could hold up his head again."

"Thanks a lot," Henry said. "But you got the end wrong. What he did afterward was he went out and stuck his head into a vat of oil to put an end to his miseries. The whole vat had to be thrown out, of course, and the master was furious." By the time Henry realized that he shouldn't say it he'd already said it.

David, however, didn't notice. "Wrong, too," he said. "He went out and raped the master's daughter, sodomized his sons, and finally his loyal hound."

"That's *sick*," Henry said.

"That's human nature for you."

"Not sick," Jon corrected. "Maybe a little pushy — "

David pointed an accusing finger at Jon. "No anti-Semitic jokes, and no double entendres, either. Remember Henry — his innocence is to be protected, I thought you told me that. I thought that mattered to you."

David always let you choose how to take what he said. Henry chose not to take this seriously. "And I want to thank you both for that," he said. "I want you to know I'm grateful."

David would have liked him to take it badly. Henry was definitely coming out the winner in this round. He leaned back on his elbows, conlented with the afternoon's work, letting Jon take over and organize them.

They called it An Entertainment, and Jon agreed to talk people into it, except for the Rabbi and Henry's father, both of whom he assigned to David. Everybody, to Henry's surprise, agreed. His mother, Jon reported, wanted to make it into a dinner party, but he refused to let her do that because they were holding it Saturday evening and the summer sun set late, and he didn't want to risk offending the Rabbi. "I'm looking forward to when the Rabbi meets your mother. Godzilla meets King Kong, or something. Frankenstein's monster meets Dracula's sisters? Didn't Dracula have sisters? Or better, do you think we could get your grandmother to come down for the evening?"

"That's not funny."

"Why not?" David wondered. "Why, if it isn't funny, might Jon think it would be, however erroneously?"

Jon didn't mind making the explanation. "Mrs. Chapin has her prejudices."

"Ah," David said.

"*And* she never sees Henry's father."

"Never? Actually never? That's interesting. Why not?"

"Yes, Hank, I've always wanted to ask — why not?"

It wasn't like Jon, forcing him in this way. If it hadn't been for David's presence, Henry would have refused to answer. "She didn't want my mother to marry him, I guess — because — I'm only guessing, nobody ever says anything — "

"Of course not," David agreed.

" — but he's not the kind of man she wanted, I guess. For my mother."

"Why not?" David asked.

"He's not a professional anything, he's not rich, he's not the same social class," and Henry was ashamed of his grandmother, "and he's not particularly successful, which — " he was ashamed of his father, too. He didn't want to think about it; there wasn't anything anyone could do, about either of them. "What about your father, Jon, what's he going to do to entertain us?"

"Pop won't say, he just says he'll do something, maybe magic tricks. But he doesn't know any magic."

David and Henry prepared the programs in the Marrs' quiet kitchen, a gift of solitary hours to Jon. Henry's job was to measure and cut the sheets of heavy paper, then make light pencil lines on it. David drew the letters of the names, using a flat thick-nibbed pen dipped into india ink. After David had completed the list of names on each sheet of paper, Henry erased his pencil marks. Henry's name headed the list but he wasn't going to worry about that, yet; he still had two days.

They worked at an easy pace to the sound of a distant piano. "How old are you going to be when you marry someone?" David asked, without looking up from the capital N he was carving in black ink onto white paper.

"No idea," Henry said, measuring. This was a strange topic for David to bring up, but he would have his reasons, Henry was pretty sure of that, and he would eventually reveal them. "I'm not sure I ever want to."

"I agree — this is no world into which to bring children." But that wasn't what Henry had been thinking of. "You must have some sense of the right age for a man, you must have thought about that, at least, what would be too young."

Henry was willing to pretend he had. "I guess pretty old, old enough to be settled, maybe twenty-five or twenty-six. So you've got a job and can support a family. But, David, why are you asking me? I never even had a girlfriend."

"I know."

Henry inhaled slowly. "Are you thinking of getting married?"

David nodded.

Henry had expected a mocking negative. He stared at Jon's cousin. "You're kidding. Who to?" He couldn't stop himself from smiling, it was such a silly game David was playing.

"Enid." For the length of a brief glance, David met Henry's eyes.

"Enid? Enid Rosen? Jon's sister?"

"That's what I said."

"But marrying Enid — why? I guess I can see it, but — "

David's patient, long-fingered hand continued to guide the pen through the letters of their names. "She'll make a man of me."

"You're actually going to do it?"

"Henry, there's something you obviously don't understand. Uncle Leo and Aunt Marya want me to, they always had it in mind — and the Rabbi, of course, because until a young man is married you can't tell what kind of trouble he'll get himself into."

"What about Enid? Does she want to?" Jon hadn't mentioned anything about Enid and David — but then Jon didn't always tell him everything. "Get married, I mean. I mean, marry you."

David put his pen down to give the question the serious thought it deserved. "She wants to fuck me. So she probably thinks she loves me. So she probably thinks she wants to marry me."

Henry's hands faltered at their task for a few seconds, then went back to work. It was, a joke. One of David's unfunny jokes.

"It's not as if she's pregnant so there's no urgency. And in fact, she's no more interested in getting pregnant than I am. Having a child, carrying it, alters a singer's voice, something to do with the rib cage and diaphragm area, she explained it to me but I wasn't paying attention — and neither would you have been, Henry. Not at the time."

Stubbornly, Henry did not ask.

"Anyway, she's always careful — you know?"

Henry didn't know and David knew that. But if David had Enid, then what was all this about whores in Boston with Jon?

David flicked a glance at Henry, and confided, "She's not much in bed anyway."

David shouldn't be talking to him like this.

"She thinks she is," David continued, "and I tell her she is — you have to do that — "

Henry wondered if that was true.

" — but she isn't much."

He wasn't going to give David the satisfaction of being shocked.

"She works too hard at it — it's so serious — she's so *heavy* about it, all that heavy breathing and grunting and moaning, she's one of those *heavy* Jews. I have a hard time getting it up for her these days, you know?"

Henry stared at David's mouth, and the row of white teeth.

"It was fun at the beginning." The mouth smiled at the memory. "Seducing her. Convincing her that she was being helplessly swept away by uncontrollable passion — "

Or jealous. Maybe jealous was what David wanted him to be.

"Getting my hands in her pants, getting her

hands in mine — I admit, that part was fun. But I'm bored now — all the gymnastics, the demands, it's boring. I'd rather . . . Do you ever wonder about Jon? Jon wouldn't get boring, sex with Jon would be fun."

"David."

"Am I shocking you?"

"Isn't that what you want to do?"

"Or is it tempting? Is it temptation? Who do you think you're kidding, Henry?"

He didn't think he was kidding himself, but what did he know? Nothing, absolutely nothing.

"Not me, you're not kidding me," David said.

"Shut up, David," Henry said.

David didn't, although he went back to the lettering. "At best, your relationship is parasite to host. Haven't you thought of that? You're the parasite," David clarified.

Henry shook his head, trapped. Because for Jon he was having the impulse to fight, to slam David around until he took everything back; and he hadn't had that impulse for Enid.

"Don't be stupid, you're not stupid — that's one thing in your favor," David said. "Otherwise, what would you see in Jon?" His cold blue eyes were amused. "Why do you think you're getting so hot and bothered?" He turned back to the paper. "Believe what you want. That's what you do anyway."

Henry would have liked to show David, if they'd take him along on one of those trips to Boston, he'd show David, he'd fuck until his eyeballs fell out, it didn't matter who. He could almost hear what Jon would say: "What a thing to do to love, Hank." Yeah, but it was what Jon had been doing, wasn't it? And who was talking about love anyway.

Henry felt sick. David made him sick, and he made himself sick. Or, maybe, David was a sickness — for everyone, in everyone — David was the sickness.

What you did with a sickness was get rid of it, kill it. Henry could, he thought, find it in himself to kill David. After all, that was what David said he wanted, wasn't it?

His hands gripped the pencil and ruler, and something gripped at his mind. The things David brought out in him couldn't have been brought out unless they were already in there.

He stood up. "Let's go. Leave that stuff, David, I'll pick up when I get back."

"But there's only one more day, because of the Sabbath. We have to get them done. There are only three more, Henry, it's not going to be bad."

"I need fresh air," Henry said. He was almost choking on his own words, having to speak them to David.

"You can go ahead. I'll just finish these up. Go ahead — I'll be fine — I won't steal anything."

Henry wasn't free to go. You didn't leave David alone, that was the unspoken understanding he had with Jon, and the Nafiches. "No," he said, "it was just — an impulse. I have trouble sticking with mechanical tasks," which was a lie and he didn't care if David knew it. It was mechanical tasks he was best at. He was a natural for the mindless mechanical task. He sat down again and picked up the pencil, reminding himself mechanically that this had nothing to do with David, it was for Jon not David, it was about Jon.

TWELVE

Next morning, the thought of going to work —
it was David of course, David again. Henry liked
working and he liked earning money —
but he didn't want to go to the restaurant that
afternoon. Just to stay away from David, for an
afternoon. At the thought, his spirits lightened.

He picked up the phone, to call in. David
answered. "It's Henry," Henry said. "Tell Mr.
Nafiche that I won't be coming to work today,
OK?" In the background, he could hear the
noises of the restaurant kitchen.

"Do you want me to tell him you're sick?"

"I want you to tell him what I asked you to."

"It's pretty busy around here. It's August,
Henry."

"I'm sorry."

"If you're sick, want me to come keep you company?"

Henry's hand tightened on the receiver, as if it could throttle the disembodied voice. "No. Thank you, anyway."

"Jon would come with me. Or Enid, I could ask her."

"No. I said no." David didn't want to see him any more than he wanted to see David. He didn't understand what David was up to and he didn't want to understand it. He just wanted not to see David for a whole day. He hung up the phone.

Henry had thought he'd use the afternoon — go for a run on the beach, memorize "The Highwayman" to recite at the Entertainment, and then see what he felt like doing in the time he had left. Instead he fell asleep on the sofa, waking late in the afternoon with a crick in his neck and a craving for chocolate. His mother had called him, to ask him to ride his bike into town for a can of tuna.

"When are you going to teach me how to drive?" he demanded.

"You never said anything about wanting to learn."

"I shouldn't have to. I'm a normal sixteen-year-old and every normal sixteen-year-old wants his license."

"Get yourself a chocolate bar while you're there," she told him. "To sweeten your disposition. I don't know why you take naps, Henry, you know you wake up cross. And I'm no happier than you are about this circus tomorrow night, so don't take it out on me thank you very much. I don't know why I let Jon talk me into it."

"My disposition doesn't need sweetening."

The other bad thing about taking naps is that when night came he wasn't tired enough to sleep. Henry lay in his bed reading, watching the clock measure off quarter hours of sleep he wouldn't get. It was nearly midnight when the phone rang.

Henry didn't even think, he jumped out of bed and ran down the stairs. He didn't even have time to put on a pair of trousers over the underpants he slept in. He didn't even take time to turn on a light. He grabbed the receiver.

"Henry? Listen, is David at your house?"

"No, not that I know of. Hold on, though, I'll go check." But he didn't have to because the kitchen lights went on and his father stood in the doorway, his bathrobe loose, his hair sticking up, sticking out, reminding Henry of an osprey's untidy nest. "Is David here?" Henry asked.

His father shook his head, and became alert. He pulled his robe close and tied it firmly.

"Not here," Henry reported to Jon. "Where is he?"

"If we knew I wouldn't have called you."

"How long has — "

"Since about nine."

"But — "

"We all thought he was with someone else."

"Jon?"

183

"Yeah, I think probably."

"I'm coming over," Henry said.

"Why?"

"I won't be long," Henry said.

"It doesn't matter."

Mr. Marr delayed Henry with a question. "What is it?"

"It's David, he's — not there, not home and — " His father nodded his head as if he'd known that all along, and was just having his knowledge confirmed. Henry ran up the stairs, got dressed, and ran down again. The kitchen was dark, the house dark and silent behind him as he wheeled his bike down the driveway.

Jon was safe now —

But what was his father doing naked under his bathrobe?

Henry hadn't really believed in it, in David's desire to kill himself. He wasn't sure he believed it now.

He wondered if he was in shock. He mounted his bike and pedaled mechanically, and the wind whistled by his ears, and he wondered if he was in some kind of mental shock.

His father said — and he seemed to understand David, seemed to like him or at least think well of him — what David did was what David didn't want to do. So if David had killed himself it was because that was now the thing he didn't want to do?

If Jon was safe, had Henry won? Had he actually beaten David?

What kind of a jerk was he, anyway — what did he think his parents did, sleeping in a double bed? Why shouldn't his father sleep nude? His mother, too.

And what business was it of his, why was he even thinking about them?

Unless it was his fault, somehow, on the phone.

And why was he going to the Nafiches', anyway?

To see Jon. But to see Jon, why? Henry didn't know why it was so important to him, and he didn't care either. He just cared about Jon, what David had done to Jon.

If David was gone, now — then what? Did he think things would go back to normal? But the only way David could be gone was to be dead. Did he want David dead? After everything David had gone through, here was Henry wishing he was dead. Because he was an unpleasant inconvenience.

Henry wouldn't have been surprised to get to the Nafiches and find David there. Find out he had been hiding in a closet to give them a good scare, or something. Because he didn't believe in David.

It wasn't that he wanted David dead. He wanted David never to have happened, that was what he wanted.

He leaned his bike against the railing and waited to catch his breath. He didn't run up the staircase, and he knew why. He could see it all, understand all of it: How the Jews could stay in Germany, because they couldn't imagine people — neighbors, co-workers, friends — turning into enemies. The property they owned, the difficulty of learning another language, because they were Germans. How they could go quietly, or even with hope, to the ghettos, to the trains and the camps and the ovens, not wanting to believe. How non-Jews — and that wasn't just the Germans either — could refuse to believe or discover what was going on, and feel innocent. How the Nazis, the SS, could treat people, do those things, with their own hands, could think they were doing something necessary or right, could live with themselves in their own innocence.

None of it was more than Henry could imagine. He knew himself. He went slowly up the wooden staircase, step by step, not in hope of escaping himself, but to spare Jon that knowledge.

The door stood open. Yellow light poured out onto the landing. He went in, down the hallway. "It's me, Henry," he called, in case anyone heard his footsteps, over the sound of moaning, and thought he was David. He had no sooner stepped into the long room than Jon, moving forward, blocked his way and shouldered him back into the hall, back toward the door. Henry had seen only a glimpse: Mrs. Nafiche at the center of the table, her hair stringy, her face mottled, her arms crossed over her chest as she

rocked gently back and forth. Enid was beside
her, pale, just watching. Mr. Nafiche was putting
a small glass of brown liquid to her lips, and
his hand stroked her head. Across the table,
with the high black windows behind him, the
Rabbi was bowed, probably in prayer.

"What happened?" Henry asked. "What can
I do?"

"We've looked all over. The car's here. But
the boat's gone. The oars, too. We've called the
Coast Guard, we've called the police." Jon stood
in the doorway, looking out over Henry's shoulder. His face was in shadows, his eyes dark and
unfathomable, his voice flat.

"I'm sorry, Jon."

Jon shrugged. Henry wanted to wrap his arms
around his friend and comfort him.

"Can I stick around? Just to wait?"

"A parable." Jon wasn't looking at Henry.
"The Parable of the Vineyards. The master had
two vineyards. The one he watered and weeded.
The other he neglected. The one flourished and
the other wasted away."

Henry waited. If there was something he could
have done he would have tried to do it. He waited
for Jon to speak.

"How are we to understand this?" Jon asked,
his eyes on some point in the darkness behind
Henry.

"I don't know."

Jon looked at him then. "I guess you better
go."

"I guess so." Henry went down the steps slowly, holding onto the handrail. He heard the door close behind him and understood, which was David's point he guessed, that he had failed his friend.

THIRTEEN

Henry awoke to a midday sun that filled his bedroom with light. He stretched, sat up. Good, he felt good, in his whole strong body. David, he remembered, was probably dead.

It wasn't certain. For certainty there had to be a corpse. He wouldn't put it past David to have set the whole thing up, to have just disappeared. David always had plenty of spending money, he could have saved it up and gone off on a vacation without telling anyone, or on a whole another life, and the Nafiches would never be sure what had happened. Or he'd come back, once he'd convinced them he'd never come back. That sounded more like David than suicide, any one of those sounded more like David. Henry turned away from the mirror and went downstairs. His parents were at the table, in the middle of some quarrel. "You knew and you didn't tell me," Henry's mother said.

His father still wore only the bathrobe, and his bony chin had stubble on it. His father hadn't gone to bed. He must have been just sitting there in that chair, all night, all morning. "It wouldn't have made any difference."

"It would have to me." She looked from his father to Henry. "It *was* important, Edwin — "

Henry's father left the room. They listened to his slow footsteps going up the stairs, then along the upstairs hall; they heard the closing of the door to his studio.

"I'm going to put off our visit to your grandmother. Do you mind?"

Henry shook his head. He was out of his depth here, and silence was his best response. He poured himself a glass of milk and sat down, listening to his mother tell his grandmother that they wouldn't be arriving tomorrow but a few days later, she'd call when she knew for sure. "No, we're all fine," she said, "but — there's been a death — " If we're lucky there has, Henry thought. "Friends of Henry's actually. You can cancel the tickets, Mother, you know you can, or invite friends to use them. I'm sorry but — " Grandy made plans and didn't like changing them; she'd be protesting the inconvenience. "No, I can't," his mother said. "I don't like to leave just now." She listened for a minute, her face a mask of politeness. "Yes, I'll call you as soon as I know. Thank you — and I truly am sorry for all the trouble. Yes, I'm looking forward to seeing you, too."

As soon as she hung up she tackled Henry. "I think you ought to tell me what's been going on."

"Nothing's been going on," Henry said. She sat down. He got up, to make himself a peanut butter and jelly sandwich. She turned in her chair, to keep her eyes on him. "It's just, there wasn't any surprise about it."

"I guessed as much. Guessed after the fact."

"They always knew he wanted to — kill himself. He always wanted to."

"Always?"

"Ever since they first found him."

"But why? You'd think, he'd be so glad to have escaped, to have survived, to have a family, relatives, to go to."

"Nobody knew, not the psychiatrists or anybody."

"What psychiatrists?"

Henry brought his sandwich to the table and sat down with his mother. "Because he lied, too — David. I think. I never believed much of what he said. He was in Germany, Mom, all through the war. He was Jewish but they hid him out with this nurse they had, they got him away, but — then he was in a DP camp and — life didn't look the same to him as it does to you."

"It couldn't, I know that, but what psychiatrists?"

"It's what he was in the hospital for — it was a psychiatric hospital."

"And I think I'm so smart," his mother said.

Even dead David could still do it. "David," Henry started to say.

"You don't like him. It's in your voice, you really dislike him."

"Have they found the body?" Henry asked.

"Your father called this morning, and Leo told him about the boat. Do you know about the boat?" Henry nodded. "Dead bodies turn up," she went on. "But, Henry, if David did want to commit suicide, why didn't he do it sooner? If he really wanted to he could have. Couldn't he? It's easy, Henry, it would have been easy for him. You know I'm right, so don't make excuses."

Henry wasn't about to make excuses for David. "Maybe he was waiting for the right time?"

"And last night was it?"

"Apparently."

His mother sat thinking. "That poor woman. And your father knew."

Henry didn't know. She'd know better than he would what his father knew.

"It's such a vicious thing to do," his mother said. "I can't even feel sorry for him. You'd think I'd at least do that, but I don't."

They stayed in the kitchen and listened to the hourly news on the radio. By late afternoon there was an announcement that a Coast Guard ship had picked up a body. Henry thought that Jon might call him up to tell him, but the phone didn't ring.

Jon didn't call Sunday, all day. Monday morning, Henry pushed the living room furniture into the center of the room and washed down the walls. Leo's, his mother reported as he lifted cans of paint out of the trunk of the car, was closed up. Henry wasn't surprised. He got to work painting; it was time somebody did something about their living room. As he worked, he listened for the phone to ring, or for Jon to come into the house.

Tuesday afternoon, he got onto his bike and rode into town. Restaurant and kitchen were dark, empty. The door into the apartment was closed. Henry knocked quietly.

It was Mr. Nafiche who opened the door. He didn't ask Henry in, although he shook hands and accepted Henry's sympathy. Mr. Nafiche wore a black band sewn around the sleeve of his suit. Henry wondered if he should have changed out of his paint-spattered jeans. "You want Jon. I'll get him for you."

As he waited out on the landing, Henry heard voices from within. Men and women were inside, speaking in heavy, solemn tones. He couldn't hear what they were saying, just the weight of their words. After a while, he saw Jon coming down the hallway, in a dress shirt and long khakis but without the armband. Mr. Nafiche pushed Jon from behind. "Go outside, you haven't been outside for days. Go take the air. But don't go far, Jon."

"I won't, Pop."

"And don't be long."

"Sure, OK."

Henry trailed behind Jon, down to the seawall. He stood beside Jon, not looking at him. Jon took deep breaths, and looked out over the water to where clouds arose from the horizon.

"I think," Jon said, without preamble, "that if we'd loved him we could have saved him. Although, one can't be certain."

Henry didn't know what to think.

"Although, I don't know about Ma, she probably did. Love him. I didn't, as you probably know — I couldn't, I didn't even like him. Except," Jon continued, "as a symbol." He studied the horizon. "As a symbol, of course, he had to die."

"What about Enid?"

"She was all over him, like some frog, but — I don't think she loved him. Do you? I was the one she asked to go with her for the abortion and — " Jon stopped. "No, it's only Ma — and I don't think she's been sober any longer than it's taken her to get into a bathrobe since he did it. Pop's going to have to get her onto something other than brandy if he doesn't want to go bankrupt."

"Is it that he hated you?" Henry asked.

"Me personally, or all of us?" Jon inquired.

Henry didn't know what to say. Jon was waiting for his answer but he didn't have to give one, because Enid called down the lawn to them, calling Jon inside. Nobody needed to tell Henry that he wasn't included.

They turned to walk back up the lawn. "Why aren't you in Boston?" Jon asked.

"My mother put it off for a couple of days, until tomorrow."

"Enjoy yourself," Jon said, moving around Enid.

Henry watched him take the stairs two at a time. What was going on with Jon? He almost asked Enid that, but she gave him no chance. "The doctors warned them," she said. "I don't understand why they're taking it like this. We knew, it's not as if we didn't know." She glared at Henry. "Do *you* think I should have married him?"

"No," he answered, appalled.

"If I had . . ."

"I don't think he even wanted you to."

"Then what did he want? You're a man, or almost; you were his friend."

"No, I'm not — I wasn't." Henry denied it, he denied everything.

"I can't ask you up," she told him.

Henry went home.

His mother greeted him with the news that they were leaving the next day for Boston. "Good," Henry said, and meant it.

"How were the Nafiches?"

"I don't know."

"And Jon?"

Jon didn't want to see me, Henry thought. "I don't know," he said. That's what it was, that cold and cerebral and Olympian tone in Jon. "OK, I guess. Hostile, unfriendly, as if it had been my fault."

"It's an isolating experience. Death. You can't expect — "

Henry nodded to show he'd heard her. He went upstairs to pack.

After dinner, they lingered around the kitchen table, reading. A knock on the door caused them to look up, look around. Henry answered it. "Mr. Nafiche." He didn't try to keep the surprise out of his voice.

Jon's father stood in the doorway, in his suit with the black band on one arm. "I'm sorry to intrude."

"It's no intrusion, Leo," Henry's mother said. "Come in. Sit down. Let me get you a cup of coffee."

"Yes, thank you," Mr. Nafiche said. He sat down heavily into a chair.

"Do you take milk? Sugar?" She put a mug down in front of him.

"No, thank you."

An awkward silence held all of them, briefly. "David," Henry's mother started.

If Henry hadn't been looking at Jon's father he wouldn't have seen the slight widening of the eyes, as if Mr. Nafiche dreaded what she might say. Mr. Nafiche cleared his throat, drank at his coffee, and announced: "I've come uninvited like this, to ask a favor."

"You don't need an invitation," Mrs. Marr said. "We'd have called, but we didn't know — "

"We understand that, and appreciate it."

"What favor?"

Mr. Nafiche looked at Henry. "You are going to Boston soon?"

"Tomorrow," Henry said. Mr. Nafiche looked tired. The flesh of his face hung heavily from its bones and his eyes looked bleary. He looked old.

"Jon told me," Mr. Nafiche explained. Henry nodded. "I wonder if Jon can go with you. To Boston."

Henry looked at his mother.

"I don't think we can do that. I'm sorry, Leo."

Which was just what she'd said to Henry, every year when he had asked the same favor; until he was old enough to be told that Jon was Jewish, and that while it might be a So What to him, it meant something to his grandmother about which he could do nothing.

"Ah, you can't." Mr. Nafiche said, his head nodding sorrowful comprehension. "I wonder why not?"

Her lips tight, she balked. She lifted her cup and drank from it. She looked at Henry. She leaned her elbows on the table and folded the fingers of her hands together.

Mr. Nafiche waited.

"Because he's Jewish," she said.

That was reason enough, if they needed reasons. What Henry needed was a chance to get away from the Nafiches, and David, and Jon, to get as far away as he could, which was his grandmother's house in Boston. He was uneasy — about everything, about Jon; he'd kept Jon safe, he'd fought with David and won, and it was over — and he needed to get away from it.

"His Jewishness comes as a surprise to you?" Mr. Nafiche asked.

"You don't need to be sarcastic."

"There are no Jews permitted in Boston?"

"We're talking about a closed world. You know that. You know what I mean. Jon wouldn't be comfortable, Leo."

"Why shouldn't he be comfortable? Henry will be there."

Henry studied his hands.

"You don't understand."

"What is it I don't understand?"

Driven to it, Henry's mother spoke forthrightly. "The anti-Semitic feeling there."

"Perhaps I do, though. Think about that. Perhaps I do understand."

"I'm sorry, Leo."

"Perhaps I also understand where such feelings lead, and how easily. For the gentile world, what else is the lesson of Dachau, of Buchenwald, of Auschwitz, of Ravensbruck." The names were like dead hands reaching up, out of the earth, long bone-fingers to catch Henry and pull him down, back into — He felt again the pity and shame, fear, guilt, disgust, anguish, like fingers clutching at him. He couldn't shake free of them, couldn't fight free, couldn't be.

"Are you blaming us for that?" Henry's mother demanded. Henry could have applauded. "Because we're not Jewish? No, Leo, you have to let me answer, you brought it up. As if only Jews died. Even in the camps it wasn't only Jews."

"I do know that, just as you have to know that for the Jews it has to be different. I do know how much you understand, Eleanor."

"I don't think I *can* understand," she admitted. "Why would you want Jon to come with us to Boston? Where he's not wanted," she explained.

And didn't want to be, Henry could have added. If something weren't wrong, Jon's father wouldn't be asking this favor. Mr. Nafiche had no way of knowing that Henry didn't want Jon in Boston anymore than Jon wanted to be there.

"You must try to see it as I do. What do I say to my son? Do I say to him, If you're Jewish it's never over? In this world, where can a Jew live? And how live, as a Jew? What do I say to my son?"

Mrs. Marr argued. "I don't see what that has to do with Jon coming to Boston."

Henry waited for Mr. Nafiche's explanation, but Mr. Nafiche had nothing to say.

This silence lasted, and lasted. It was Henry's

father who broke it. "It's not just Jews, Ellie. Not just Jon. It's everybody. It's Henry, too."

"What do you mean by that?"

"I mean," he said slowly, "that Henry also has to live. In this world, as Leo said."

She got up to pour out another round of coffee, and didn't sit down with them again.

"I ask you, please, to take him with you," Mr. Nafiche said. "I ask you, please, for my son."

Mrs. Marr stood there, unable to decide. "Henry? No, never mind — I won't ask you. Henry," she told Jon's father, "would walk through fire in bare feet if your Jon asked him to." Henry wondered, imagining flames and coals on his bare soles — and he wasn't sure he could count on himself.

"My Jon would walk with him."

He wasn't sure he could count on Jon, either.

"I know," Mrs. Marr said.

"You and I should pray that the necessity doesn't arise," Jon's father said.

"I don't like the idea of taking him to Boston, Leo. I don't like it for Jon."

"Even so, you will do it?"

"I don't want to."

"But you will?"

She wanted to say no. "I'll ask, I'll do that. If my mother says it's all right with her, then we will. But I'm not convinced it's a good thing for Jon, Leo." Nobody seemed to be concerned about Henry, he noticed. "No, stay here, we'll have it settled." She went to the phone and placed the call. "Hello, Mother. No, we're still coming tomorrow, late afternoon, but I have a question: May Henry bring a friend?" She listened at the phone. "That's fine then. We'll see you tomorrow, around four?"

Mr. Nafiche said nothing more than "Thank you." He shook hands with each one of them, and left.

Jon was waiting for them the next morning, sitting on the bottom stair with a suitcase beside him. He put the suitcase into the rear seat, then got in beside it and shut the door, before Henry could decide whether to move back there with him. Henry's mother drove away.

"Pop asked me to tell you again thank you for having me," Jon said to Henry's mother. "He'd have been there himself but my mother needed him upstairs."

"I hope you'll have a good time," Mrs. Marr answered.

They looked at one another in the rearview mirror as they spoke.

"Well, we thought it might be good for Ma to have me out of the house for a while."

"And if you don't like it, we can get you back home. There wouldn't be any problem about that, all you have to do is say so. If you want to."

"Pop already told me. Don't worry, I understand."

Understand what? Henry almost asked, but he didn't, and by the time he had turned his head around again to speak to Jon, Jon was leaning back into a corner of the seat, apparently asleep.

FOURTEEN

The Chapin house sat on a long ridge of land, much of which Henry's grandmother owned. The graveled driveway crunched beneath the tires. Tall trees formed an archway. Jon, awake again, looked out the window, at the slopes of lawn and his first glimpse, as the car rounded a curve, of the long stone house, as solid as if it had grown out of the rocks that shaped the hills behind it. Jon looked at Henry, his mouth pursed in a soundless whistle. Henry shrugged, embarrassed.

Mrs. Marr stopped the car in front of the house. The door opened and Mrs. Chapin stepped out, flanked by two servants, one to take the luggage, the other to drive their car away and put it out of sight. Full of a sense of ceremony, Henry slowly mounted the three steps.

He kissed his grandmother's cheek twice a year, once on arriving and once on leaving. This bright afternoon, he noticed that he no longer had to reach up to her cheek. She looked straight at him; he looked at her. His grandmother was tall for a woman and dressed, as always, in muted colors. The pearls on her chest glowed. "You're beginning to grow," she told Henry. "Good. Chapin men are always tall."

When his grandmother smiled, her teeth gleamed. Grandy was proud of her teeth. Chapins had good teeth; they were buried with their own teeth. Henry smiled back at her, revealing his own good teeth.

"This is my friend, Jon Nafiche," he said, stepping aside. Jon shook Mrs. Chapin's hand, on which diamonds and emeralds glittered. "It's an honor to meet you," Jon said.

Mrs. Chapin had to look up to study Jon's features. She let go his hand and held his eyes. "They didn't tell me you were Jewish."

Henry's mother expelled air in a noisy breath. You had to hand it to his grandmother, Henry thought; and he wondered what Grandy would do now.

But it was Jon who made the move, saying mildly, "They didn't tell me you were rich."

There was an extended silence. "Mother," Mrs. Marr protested and Mrs. Chapin stood aside to let them enter the cool, high-ceilinged home.

Henry led Jon right up to the bedroom they would share, up the polished staircase with its dark oriental runner, around the landing that overlooked the hallway, and along another rug to what had once been his uncle William's room. This was the east wing. Their room faced north over the side lawns and gardens, and east down the gradual slope of the countryside to a distant silver gleam of river. A few rooftops were visible, each ringed by trees.

Their suitcases had been set out on racks and opened to facilitate unpacking. Jon stood looking out a window and then turned to consider the room, and to watch Henry unpack into a heavy mahogany bureau. "I don't know, Henry, she's not too excited about me."

You had to hand it to Jon, too. "That's an understatement. I had no idea, Jon." It was only for a week; it was only Jon — it would be OK.

"I hate to think what she's saying to your mother right now."

"Un-unh, Jon." Henry looked him in the eye. "Grandy doesn't say things behind your back."

"The impeccable Chapins, is that it?" Jon started to unpack into a bureau that matched Henry's. Henry stifled the impulse to answer "Yes, exactly" to the tone of Jon's voice. What was so wrong with being a Chapin anyway?

"But, Henry," Jon cried behind him. "That means she'll say it to my face." Henry smiled, not in a kindly fashion. "I'm not sure a mere change of venue is worth all this."

"All what?" Henry asked. "Check out the bathroom, Jon."

Emerging from his tour of inspection, Jon's only comment was, "Those tiles are marble."

The tiles were marble, to hold the heat of the shower water, and the towels were thick, soft. Henry came out of the shower feeling wrapped around in comfort as thick and soft as the towel. When he went into their bedroom to get dressed, Jon was lying on the bed. "You ought to have a shower," Henry offered.

"Is there any hot water left? Wait, don't tell me, Chapins never run out of hot water."

"All right, I won't tell you."

Dressed up, dressed out in suits and ties and polished shoes, Henry and Jon descended the staircase and joined Henry's mother and grandmother, also changed for the evening meal, in a long living room. The two women sat turned toward one another at opposite ends of a sofa. Henry sat in one of a pair of wing chairs. Jon took the other.

After five minutes, Henry found himself wondering why he had pestered his mother to invite Jon along in previous years. After five minutes Henry was entirely on edge, sitting stiff in the chair, gripping his glass of ginger ale as if — if he loosened his fingers — it would fly off into somebody's face, his grandmother's stiff and formal and unrelenting, or Jon's where he sat looking like some diplomat, some foreign diplomat, with his legs stretched out, his ankles crossed, relaxed, at diplomatic ease.

A silver platter sat on the low table in front of the sofa, filled with concentric circles of artichoke leaves, each leaf tipped with a tiny pink shrimp nestled on a dollop of curried mayonnaise. "None for me, thanks," Jon said, when the plate was offered to him; what he did not say hovered unspoken on the air.

Grandy made conversation. "What does your father do?"

"He's a cook," Jon answered from the depths of his chair.

Henry's mother looked at Henry. Henry shifted in his seat.

"A cook." Grandy hesitated. "What does he cook?"

"In a restaurant," Jon told her.

"Ah. Is this the restaurant where you've been employed?" she asked Henry.

"Yes." Henry tried to catch Jon's eye. "Mr. Nafiche owns it."

"I see," his grandmother said. "Is it," she searched for the correct word, "kosher?"

"No, ma'am, it's French," Jon said.

"Surely there are French kosher cooks," Grandy snapped.

"I expect there are," Jon agreed, smiling pleasantly.

Jon wasn't making it easy. Grandy was wearing her good manners like an evening dress; Henry could almost see her hands smooth down the skirts of her good manners as she turned to her daughter. "I don't know how these boys are going to amuse themselves for a week. Do you have any plans for them?"

Henry's mother caught Henry's eye.

"We'll be fine," Henry said.

"Because usually," Grandy told Jon, "Henry spends his days at the Club, where he swims, or finds a game of golf with one or more of the young people."

Henry avoided Jon's eye and leaned forward to grab up one of the artichoke leaves. He took his time about scraping the meat off against his teeth, and chewing, and swallowing. His grandmother had to know that he almost never went to the Club, she must at least have noticed that there were no bills coming in for guest privileges or lunches. He supposed she might think that he went there, because she had no idea that anyone might do anything else; and it certainly wasn't like her to tell lies so she probably did; but that was just because she wanted to think that was what he did.

"I packed swimming trunks," Jon assured her.

Mrs. Marr spoke up. "Henry doesn't play golf, Mother."

"He doesn't? Why ever not? I've given you free use of my membership at Chatham."

"I do," Jon volunteered. Henry laughed aloud. His grandmother was asking for trouble, with Jon.

"What is amusing?" she asked Henry.

"He's teasing you." Although, teasing was the

wrong word. Baiting was more like it.

Henry didn't know why he had thought it would be fun to have Jon around in Boston. Conversation was like a duel with rapiers, parry and thrust. Sometimes it seemed that Grandy was in control, and sometimes it seemed to be Jon who was pressing the advantage. Nothing Henry or his mother did could sway either one of them from the game of ambiguously worded questions, doubled-edged answers, which they played out in the living room and then at the dinner table. Jon should have known what Grandy was like. Henry had told him, often enough. But Jon was never this way, humorless. That was it, exactly, humorless.

They talked about the cream of spinach soup (". . . if only your cook had used fresh chicken stock, not canned . . .") and *The Stranger* ("He mistakes *angst* for *nous*, despair for wisdom, or am I showing my age?), architecture (" . . . the difference between houses built with the eye to future generations and places inhabited by people whose highest ambition, or is it hope? is to survive to the next day"), and history ("It is surely significant that our ancestors signed the Mayflower Compact before anyone set foot on shore, that the social contract — the first instance of a social contract made with full and present consciousness — preceded society"). Henry ate his sturdy way through roast beef, oven-roasted potatoes, Yorkshire pudding, green beans. Nobody asked for his thoughts. Jon and Grandy left no room for anyone else to say anything.

"This is a good dinner," Jon remarked, before returning to his topic (his topic was Kafka). "A very good dinner. Of course, Kafka was a Jew, which gives him a peculiar perspective." He watched Grandy to see how she would answer that.

Henry could have told him: Head on. "You think he would have a deeper understanding of suffering. In the particular case, the suffering of alienation felt by the unassimilated individual, within a fixed hierarchical society."

Jon ignored the polysyllabic challenge. "Oh, well, suffering. The Jews seem to think they've cornered the market on suffering, but I'll tell you," Jon told her, "I don't think they're a patch on the Russians."

Henry didn't know what Jon thought he was up to. His grandmother's mouth was a thin line; she didn't want to talk about anything, not with Jon.

In the darkness of their bedroom that night, Jon's voice remarked, "This is the place where you ought to be living. David would have loved it."

"David didn't love anything."

"Do you think that? Do you really think that?"

Henry couldn't tell if Jon was being sarcastic or sincere, so he ignored the question. "I hope you're enjoying yourself."

210

"Yeah, I am. Although I don't know if your grandmother is. Are there any other grandchildren?"

"You know there aren't."

Their disembodied voices floated in the unlit air.

"So you'll inherit."

"Not likely."

"You mean," Henry heard a rustling of sheets, and heard that Jon had turned to face him, "she's not only going to keep her life here to herself, within this no-man-land's moat of money — but she's going to do — what? Give it to a cat farm?"

"Ease up, Jon, OK? I couldn't live in this house anyway."

"Why not? You fit right in."

"Then you're not looking clearly. You're the one who looks at home, bandying double-edged sentences, reclining in the Queen Anne chairs."

"Me? You're kidding. As soon as I stepped out of the car, I could feel my forelocks growing. The creases fading from all of my trousers. What you've seen tonight is my famous goy imitation."

Henry sputtered, told Jon to shut up and go to sleep.

Jon ignored him. "You're right to want to go into the military," he said. "I look at those portraits, all those fat-faced Chapins, self-satisfied . . . They were all nobodies, Henry, empty waistcoats, stuffed with straw, I mean literally nobodies, or maybe no-selves? I used to think you just talked about the military to — you

211

know — show your father. Either way, I can see it now."

"I'm glad to have your approval." Henry didn't conceal his resentment.

"Oh, you don't, that's not what I meant at all."

"You know, Jon," Henry said, pulling the blanket up over his shoulders to put finish to the conversation, "you know who you sound like."

"No. I don't. Who? Who do I sound like, Henry?"

FIFTEEN

The next morning, although Jon announced his willingness to go over to The Club — the two words given pronounced reverence — and knock off a few holes, Mrs. Chapin arranged for the car to take the boys into Boston, gave Henry money for lunch, and instructed them — looking at a point in the air between them as they stood on her doorstep — to see historic sites, see the Alcott and Revere houses, see the Old North Church, see Concord, see Lexington. Henry, made a little giddy at the frontality of Jon's attack, chanted, "By the rude bridge that arched the flood, Their flag to April's breeze unfurled."

His grandmother waited impatiently.

"Here once," Henry declaimed, "the embattled farmers stood, And fired the shot heard 'round the world." He took a bow, although there was no applause.

"Ah, but, Henry," Jon said. "The foe long since in silence slept; Alike the conquerer silent sleeps; And Time the ruined bridge has swept, Down the long stream that seaward creeps."

Grandy opened her mouth to say something but Jon beat her to it. "How are we to understand this?" he asked. Before she could answer, Jon hustled Henry into the back of the car.

Why did Jon always have to best him, Henry asked himself. He didn't understand what Jon was up to, except Jon wasn't besting him. Jon was just being Jon, which was better than being Henry. Except Jon never used to make Henry feel stupid and thick of mind.

They returned late in the afternoon, to an early dinner before a concert. At the table Jon discussed twentieth century music and composers with Mrs. Marr. Grandy, as he had ascertained early in the discussion, like Henry, knew nothing about the subject. "Not even your son-in-law's work," Jon commented and went on to ask Henry's mother about Ives, and Cage, Bartok and atonality.

On Friday Jon expressed his interest in going to The Club for a swim, but Grandy pressed money into Henry's hand and told the chauffeur to take them into Cambridge. "It might rain," she said, indicating the cloudy sky, "and moreover, all the Chapins have gone to Harvard, or Radcliffe."

"How well-rounded," murmured Jon, who wasn't letting anything pass.

"What are your college plans?" Grandy asked.

"Oh, Harvard, of course," Jon said without hesitation. "It's Henry you should be thinking about." He climbed into the waiting car.

The big car rolled noiselessly down the drive, Henry and Jon locked into enforced companionship by the thick window that separated them from the front seat. "What did you mean by that crack?" Henry demanded. "Don't you think I can get into Harvard?"

"Of course you can, but who's going to pay the bills? I ask you that."

"What do you mean?"

"Don't you ever think? By rights — if we use that term very loosely, which is another argument for another day — but by rights you should be at Groton now, or St. Paul's, Choate, at whatever prep school the Chapins have established as the Family Institution. Exeter, I bet it's Exeter. Instead, you're at Orleans High. Don't you ever think about that?"

"No. Why should I?"

Jon just looked at him.

"That's where you are."

"Yeah, but I'm a Jew. Henry, sometimes I don't know about you. No, wait, a little goyish thinking here, I can do it — I'm doing it pretty well so far, don't you think? It's because of your father. Isn't it?" He jabbed Henry in the ribs with a finger. "Because he's alive and her son isn't. Because he's much older than your mother, and he's not being a success — so it wasn't a good match for a Chapin. Because she made up her mind years ago to have something against him." Jon watched Henry's face. "There it is again, that old Chapin loyalty."

Jon made loyalty sound like a vice. "What do you have against her? You're not even acting like yourself, Jon. You bait her, almost all the time. That's not like you."

"A parable," Jon said. Henry almost groaned. "The Parable of the Prisoner. There was a prisoner, alone in a cell with one tiny barred window up high on the wall. In his solitude, the prisoner befriended — if that's the appropriate word — a cockroach. He would give the creature part of his daily bread, and talk to it. Sometimes he let it crawl over his body. Sometimes he would trap it under the empty soup bowl and leave it there for hours, to study its panic. Once he removed a leg, and it made him laugh to see the queer hobbled gait. Until he got used to it."

"What is that supposed to mean? Do you mean Grandy is a prisoner? Or you, because you're the one that is baiting her. What is it supposed to mean if the prisoner dismembered the cockroach?"

"It kept him alive," Jon said. "Maybe it kept

him sane. And who knows what the relationship meant to the cockroach."

"No," Henry said. "This time you are way off beam."

"Think about it, Henry. Keep thinking about it, because you haven't even scratched the surface of my intentions. You know, this is a very educational vacation I'm having — seeing how the other half lives, checking out the opposition. Seeing your heritage close up, too. It's a wonder you're a human being," Jon said. "I can see why your father keeps clear of this rampant hypocrisy."

"Are you trying to be offensive?" Henry asked.

"Yes," Jon said, grinning. "Do I take it I am succeeding?"

Henry couldn't even smile back: He had lost Jon, or something, Jon was lost to him, they were lost to one another. David had done this. David had won out after all. "Damn David," Henry said.

He hadn't meant to say it aloud. Or maybe, he wondered, doubting his own motives, he had.

"David is dead and has nothing to do with it," Jon told him, like a cannon blast full in his face.

Henry turned away.

That evening, in the long dining room, after Mrs. Chapin and Mrs. Marr had discussed the life histories of the women they had lunched with at The Club, their husbands and where the husbands worked, their marriages and children, where their children were at school and how they were doing, Jon took adavantage of a gap in the conversation to ask Mrs. Chapin, "What about Henry? You remember, your grandson, Henry? What about where he is?"

"Henry's right here," she answered, deliberately stupid. Henry didn't blame her. He felt like telling Jon just to shut up.

"Yes, precisely," Jon said, "But he's more importantly not there, *there* being wherever the Chapin boys go for their preparatory education. Where did your brother go to school, Mrs. Marr?"

"Exeter, Jon. It doesn't matter," she said.

Jon grinned across the table at Henry. Then he turned to his hostess. "Shouldn't Henry be at Exeter?"

"Jon, please," Mrs. Marr said. Jon ignored her.

"I don't see why." Mrs. Chapin dismissed the question.

"Because he's intelligent," Jon answered, as if she has asked. "Because he's a Chapin."

Henry sat there and felt like a fool, a jerk, a real asshole. His grandmother put her fork down and stared at Jon, not bothering to conceal her distaste. "I cannot believe that the education of my grandson is any of your business."

"You're absolutely right," Jon agreed. "Except — if you'll forgive me?"

Grandy waited, but Jon outwaited her.

"It seems to me I've forgiven you a great deal already," she said carefully.

"I appreciate that. So, why not one more vulgarity?"

She pursed her lips, thought, and answered, "I wasn't aware of forgiving you vulgarity."

She had him there, Henry thought.

Jon smiled. "Point taken, point well taken, and I apologize. Still, I don't think you know about Henry, seeing him only once a year, and in this house. I don't think you know him. For example, do you know what kind of pajamas he wears?"

"Oh, Jon," Mrs. Marr said quietly, "let it drop."

"Yeah," Henry echoed. He didn't know what Jon was after, and he didn't like being used as a stick to beat his grandmother with.

Mrs. Chapin held up her hands to brush away the interference. Emerald stones glowed in the candlelight and the facets of diamonds glittered. "It's all right, Ellie." She hesitated, then answered Jon. "I suspect that, like most young men, Henry sleeps nude, or as close to it as he can manage."

It was so unexpected a thrust that Henry laughed aloud. His grandmother, pleased with herself and him, smiled at him. "She's got you, Jon, and you know it."

"I know young men," Mrs. Chapin said. "I had two brothers, and a son. I'm not as narrow as you take me for."

"I never said you were narrow," Jon countered. "I only said you didn't know Henry."

Mrs. Chapin didn't say anything to that, but she looked at Henry with more interest than she had ever shown before. Jon, apparently satisfied, took up his knife and fork. He cut himself a bite of braised duckling. "Where are your brothers now, what do they do?" he asked. "Then I'll tell you about mine," he offered. He put the bite into his mouth.

Mrs. Chapin's face closed off and she withdrew behind it. "Both dead. One in the first World War, one on the operating table. A routine appendectomy," she added. "He was fifteen."

Grandy's voice gave her away. Jon put his fork down and his knife. Henry watched him try not to respond. Watching, Henry saw Jon fail. His hand moved along the table toward the woman and Henry felt — as if it were a tangible wave — compassion flow from Jon to the aging woman who sat out of reach. "I'm so sorry," Jon said. He sounded like himself for the first time in days. "Nobody gets through unscathed, do they?"

"Don't mouth platitudes at me, young man. What would you know about it?" Grandy demanded, rejecting his sympathy, his hand — rejecting him.

"No, Grandy, listen — "

"Something," Jon interrupted. His hand,

drawn back, rested at apparent ease beside his plate, his voice was once again emotionless. "I know something of it. You'll require proof, of course, Chapins don't take anything on faith. Proof forthcomes."

"Really," Mrs. Chapin objected. "Really, Ellie." But Jon's voice continued.

"My paternal grandparents, Helen and Baptiste Nafiche. My father's brother, Louis; his wife, Mimi; two cousins Claude and Rachelle, aged seven and ten. Young, you must admit, they were young. Also my mother's first husband. Also her sister, Clarisse Bach; Clarisse's husband, Otto; and their four children, one a promising violinist — although that is admittedly hearsay evidence. My aunt, Sofie Steintodt; her husband, Herman; and three of their four children, Elisabet, Joshua, Anna." He spoke the names slowly. "My maternal grandparents, the Feders, Seiglinde, and Hershel. And I think we might also include David, my cousin David Steintodt, the only survivor, who died last week. David was twenty. Although since he killed himself, you might argue that he's not entirely relevant."

Grandy would have to take care of herself, Henry thought; it was Jon he was watching. He waited, but Jon had finished.

Nobody said anything. Jon's hostility filled the room.

"And I think, by the way," Jon said,

"that I'm glad David finally did it."

At either end of the table the women drew in deep breaths of air. They seemed to flutter in the candlelight, off at the periphery of Henry's vision. He leaned his arms on the table, bringing his body closer to Jon where he sat in his dark suit, his eyes avoiding Henry's.

"Jon?" Henry asked. "But, Jon. There's no reason why you shouldn't be glad." This, he had done some thinking about; this he could speak of. "David was going after you. You especially. You know that Jon. It was you he was after."

"There's a legend," Jon answered him. Their eyes were locked now; Henry's glance ricocheted back at him. Somebody, either Grandy or his mother, spoke. Jon told the story:

"After the Red Sea had parted and washed away the army of Pharaoh to their deaths, and the people of Moses proceeded safely on into the wilderness, the angels in heaven wanted to make a song, a song of celebration and triumph. But the Master of the Universe, blessed be his name, checked them. 'The work of my hands is drowned in the sea,' He said. 'And you would offer me a song!' "

Henry saw then, or thought he saw, in that thick air the candlelight barely penetrated, why Mr. Nafiche had sent Jon away. Understanding hammered at him, hurting him. The women had subsided and waited intensely. This wasn't the kind of conversation you had at a Chapin dinner table, but he was going to, because Jon was giving him a chance.

"There's a flaw in the analogy," Henry said. "If there are parallels, then the Jews should have been led out of the camps. Which raises," he had to say this, even though he didn't want to, "certain difficult questions."

Jon's face dismissed what Henry had said. Henry thought further.

"There's another flaw."

Jon's eyebrows questioned him.

"You're not God," Henry pointed out.

"There is that," Jon said. His voice was unruffled but his eyes gave him away. At least, Henry thought, he'd amused Jon. "You mean to say I'm only human."

"Something like that. It loses in the translation."

" 'And death shall have no dominion,' " Jon quoted. "Is that where you're leading?"

All of the attention was focused on Henry. He could feel his mother's sharp glance and Grandy's speculative one; he could see Jon's. He brushed those perceptions aside. It was so complicated, so damnably complicated and impossible to simplify into words.

"No," he started. "That's not what I mean."

Jon looked doubtful, as if he knew better. Henry hurried on before he lost contact with Jon again.

"What I mean is — remember you told me once, with quotes — "

"Everything I tell you has quotes."

" — that we have to choose, choose life or choose death?"

"I remember vividly," Jon said, but his voice belied the word. "What I didn't tell you is that choosing life is like choosing — to have your liver taken out daily by an unskilled eagle. Or perpetual crucifixion."

"Yes, you did. You did already tell me that," Henry answered. "What is it, are you afraid?"

He had surprised Jon, for once. Jon for once had nothing to say. Henry pressed his advantage. "David was afraid of everything, winning and losing, getting and spending, crime and punishment — everything. Except dying."

"I think," Jon said slowly, "he might have been afraid of dying most of all."

"Let me finish," Henry insisted. "The plain fact is that David chose death. And as far as I'm concerned, that's OK, that's even fair enough. He had the right and I can even see why he wanted to. No, I really can, whether you believe me or not. But he was trying to choose death for you, too, he's trying to force you to that now. And he has no right," Henry said. The fierceness of his own voice frightened him, at what it betrayed. He swallowed slowly before going on. "I think he figured out how you'd react, how you'd feel — he was really smart, Jon, he was a master psychologist, you lived with him, you must know that — and that's one reason he did it. Not the only reason — I wouldn't ever say that — but I don't think even David could sort it all out. But you have to be glad he's dead, because you're human, but that's only part of what you're feeling. But if you don't honor that feeling, too, then you're trying to be God. You can't try to be God without choosing death, as a human."

Henry considered what he had said. "That's what I mean. Maybe it is 'And death shall have no dominion,' but only in a way. Because death does have dominion, you can't lie to yourself about that, and history does, too. But only its own dominion, it doesn't have to have more, we don't have to let it."

Jon looked at him, looking into his eyes. "That's what you really think?" He warned Henry, "Because I trust you, Hank. You, I trust, and I'll believe you."

No, Henry thought, don't trust me, don't believe me. "Yes," he said, meeting Jon's eyes. The lie sickened him.

"OK," Jon said, speaking casually, smiling easily.

"OK what?" Henry insisted.

"OK maybe," Jon told him. "That's as far as I'm willing to go right now. Maybe it *is* a blessing to survive."

Henry wouldn't have gone that far, even with Jon. Henry knew that like David, he was false,

false to the heart. David at least was innocent of what he was false to; Henry wasn't, he knew what and he knew why. The long silence went on, and went on, until Mrs. Chapin spoke.

"The camps. The concentration camps."

Jon turned his head slowly. "The death camps."

"It was stupid of me," Mrs. Chapin said.

"Not stupid," Jon told her. "Careless."

She stood up then, folding her napkin neatly beside her plate. "I'll say good night now. But I think I'll find — as I consider it — that I owe you an apology, Jon. You are — as you know — a formidable young man." She left the room in stately haste.

They watched her go. "I don't know what you think you're doing, Jon," Mrs. Marr said. "Or you, Henry, I don't — "

"Mom," Henry said. "Please," he asked her.

She excused herself and followed her mother out of the room.

After a long time, Jon spoke. "I've been a rotten guest, haven't I? How angry at me are you?" Henry shook his head, he wasn't. "I shouldn't have come, I told Pop. I shouldn't have talked to her like I have, I'm not proud of myself in case you're wondering. From now on, I'll behave myself. I promise, every minute. Charming, I'll be utterly charming and irresistible."

Well, that sounded like Jon, Jon sounded like himself. Henry roused himself to answer. "Yeah, but what about Grandy?"

"She's tougher than you give her credit for," Jon told him. "She's kind of a tough old coot. I think I'll like her, what do you think, Hank? Should I like her?"

That night, when Henry was convinced Jon had been long asleep, his voice floated across the darkness. "What do you think, Hank? I bet she takes us to The Club."

"Grandy? Never."

"How much will you put on it. A dollar? I'm putting my money on your grandmother. What about you?"

"Go to sleep," Henry said. "You need your energy for tomorrow."

Jon was quiet for a while, then spoke again. "Did you ever hear David laugh?"

Henry thought about this. "Maybe once. I never saw him cry either, Jon."

"I've never seen you cry, Henry."

"No, you haven't."

"Hank?" Jon asked, turning over with a rustling of sheets.

"Go to sleep," Henry advised him. "I'm trying to."

After a while, Jon said, "We've had it easy, you know that. Do you ever think of how easy we have it? Do you think we'd do any better than other people have? That's what I'm afraid of, Henry."

"This," Henry asked, "is easy?" He felt as if over the last months he'd been blown apart into little fleshy fragments, and then stitched together, and he'd never move again without pain.

"Relatively speaking, yeah."

Henry could see what Jon meant and be glad Jon meant it, but David had changed all that for him. David had made it impossible for Henry to go back, to who he had been and to what he and Jon had been.

"Doesn't it scare you?" Jon insisted.

"Yes," Henry said, into the darkness.

He wondered if, if he had known what it was going to cost him, he'd have undertaken to take on David. He didn't know. He'd like to think he would have, but he wouldn't bet on himself. That was all right, he thought, smiling to himself in the dark, since he hadn't known and therefore attempted it. Since he hadn't and had — so to speak — the whole question of *if* became hypothetical, and unanswerable. If unanswerable — he worked it out — then there was nothing to be gained by thinking about it, which was a kind of blessing.

"Hank? What are you thinking?"

"About the futility of questioning the unanswerable," Henry said, certain that Jon wouldn't understand.

"Ah," Jon said, his voice rich with laughter. "I myself was wondering which shirt I should wear when we're taken to The Club. I probably shouldn't go so far as a stripe, do you think? It would be an occasion for maximum understatement, wouldn't it?"

"You sound like you're counting on it."

"Well and why not? Sufficient unto the day is the hope thereof — as it isn't written. What harm can hope do?" Jon asked rhetorically. Henry wasn't about to answer that question.

1967

He washed his hands, rinsed them in scalding water, and washed them again. Jon asked more from people than he had any right to expect. What Jon didn't know was that Henry still had a choice; he could have Fowler take over, let Fowler be the one to run the risks, let some stranger do the damage. Let Fowler to be the one to operate.

To take the scalpel into his hand and cut, Henry specified, cut and then pull back an apron of Jon's flesh. To bore holes into Jon's skull and saw through the living bone. To take a section of Jon's skull and prise it up until it cracked. And that . . . he could have laughed . . . was before the hard part began. That was just prep.

Jon simply assumed Henry would do it. "You won't screw up, that's not your kind of mistake.

Your kind of mistake is being too cautious. Do me a favor, Henry, don't be too cautious, don't dawdle. Be brilliant." Fowler was good; nobody at Special Surgical wasn't good. The terrible thing was that Henry was better.

Henry had told Jon the situation — "Shrapnel, and bones, and one large piece that's deeper" — and the procedures — "First we'll shave your head" — but not the dangers Jon lay under if he survived the operation. Jon didn't ask about them either. All Jon asked was, "Will I look like Yul Brynner?" as if — as if it was some game. Henry almost walked out then, walked away from it, walked away from Jon, who always asked too much of him.

Six hours later — six hours and twenty-three minutes, he noted — he'd finished. The nurse wrapped Jon's head, covering all but the yellowy-brown antiseptic stain that spread out from under the bandages down over the cheekbones and ear and neck. The bandages concealed the naked flesh, swollen, wounded, crisscrossed with black stitches, and concealed the closed eyes. Henry's hands were coated with blood as was his apron; behind him, trays were mounded with bloody instruments, trephine and rongeurs, needles and wires, bloody cloths and swabs, the blood smell crowding up against the smell of antiseptic. Only the laser knife was unmarked. The nurse wheeled Jon out of the theater. Henry, almost too tired to get out without being wheeled himself, nodded to Fowler and the rest. "Good work."

Live or die, that was true. You had to remember that. What you always needed to know, and always couldn't, was whether you had done the best possible.

"You went in fast," Fowler observed.

"He asked me to."

"He's not a surgeon, is he?"

"No. A friend," Henry admitted.

"Jesus, Marr. How could you — I'm not complaining, if you'd left it to me we'd still be in there, with another three or four hours to go, but — So he's a friend of yours? Looks a lot like Yul Brynner, doesn't he?"

Henry could have laughed.

Henry sat beside Jon's bed in postop. A surgeon should be there — and especially here and now Henry should — when his patients struggled up from anesthesia; or died; or defined whatever no man's mental land they'd be inhabiting now that medicine and history were through with them. Only half of the beds were occupied that afternoon. Voices around him moaned, cried out, wept, vomited; nurses in sneakers moved around behind him.

"Hank?" Jon's voice was thick, weak.

"Here," Henry answered. He put his fingers onto the bony shoulder. "How do you feel?"

Jon's mouth moved, trying to form words. "Shit."

Coherent thought, maybe. "That's good," Henry said, his chest tight with anxiety, or relief.

"Mas-o — " Jon bit down on his lip. His stretched skin looked gray, his mouth flaccid; he moved restlessly on the bed.

"Stay quiet," Henry said. "I've got medication."

"Strong," Jon asked.

Henry administered the shot and then held Jon's hand against pain that brought beads of sweat out on his neck. "I tell you . . . when Laurie . . . had Sofie . . ." Jon was unconscious before Henry could answer, "Seven times."

By the next morning, Jon was fully conscious.

"Good morning," Henry greeted him.

"Is it? Morning, I mean. I'm not ready to deal with the question of the good." The half-faced figure flat on the bed reminded Henry of an insect.

"How do you feel?"

"Like I'll never have the courage to try to lift my head off this pillow," Jon answered. "I feel too good for how bad I feel. What are you giving me?"

"Morphine."

"Henry," Jon protested.

"We're buying time," Henry told him. "Don't worry, we won't — overdo it."

"You do and I'll kill you. Then myself. I mean it. I know how now, Henry."

"You've lost an eye," Henry told him.

"Not that I mind feeling so good. Not that I don't trust you. But I think one chemically dependent relative is all children should have to put up with, don't you?"

"We've learned to be careful," Henry said.

They stood in a ragged line at the foot of Jon's bed, three of them. All wore hospital pajamas, blue and white striped, sizes too large. Their necks were narrow columns, fragile for the weight of heads. At Henry's approach they turned away, with a rustling of paper slippers. Jon slept. The three men looked, as Henry followed them and they moved along the Intensive Care ward and out into the corridor, as if they were fifteen or sixteen and weren't yet sure what to do with these bodies they were inhabiting. He called, "Hey," and they turned around. Their faces were not young.

"What do you want with Jon?"

"You mean him in the bed?"

"Are you a doctor?"

Henry nodded.

"A shrink?"

"They said it was OK if we went for a walk. We didn't talk to him, we didn't hurt him."

"I'm the surgeon," Henry said.

"We didn't wake him up."

"They said he's gonna be OK."

"We think he might," Henry said. "He's got a chance. But — "

"It wouldn't be fair if he wasn't."

"Fair. Jesus. You're really an asshole some-times."

"You were in the camp," Henry guessed.

"It's OK for us to just look. Nobody said we couldn't."

"It's OK," Henry said. "But what did you want?"

They looked at each other, to find the answer.

"Just to see."

Henry nodded, as if he understood.

"He'd clown around, see."

"They didn't speak much English."

"He'd pretend to translate for us."

"Some of that was — pretty funny. If you can believe anything being funny."

"I can," Henry said and he guessed he could. He couldn't imagine it, but he could believe it.

"They put him in this basket — and we all — we marched, we had to march around him and watch him — and — "

"We don't have to tell him about this."

"Yeah, he's not a shrink, we don't have to answer his questions."

"We didn't touch anything."

"He was always up to something — the poor bastard."

Their eyes searched one another out, to reassure.

"Yeah."

"I'm hungry."

"Let's go back."

"When he comes to, Doc, say hey for us. Will you?"

"Sure," Henry promised.

They moved away, quarreling.

"You shouldn't put a man in a cage. Like that, all naked, and all."

"He didn't mind."

"Oh, yeah? You've got it all wrong, buddy. He wouldn't have made it through another day."

"You always say that."

"Are you giving odds?"

"He'd never have made it. If they hadn't found out where we were and come to get us out, they'd have gotten him, too."

"Don't say that. Say that again and I'll get you, when they get us out of here."

"Hey, what do you mean *when*, buddy."

"OK. OK. *If*."

After a week Jon was shifted into the general wards. Henry oversaw the move, not because he needed to. "We'll keep you curtained off for a couple of days," he told Jon.

"What I want to know is, why medical people feel it necessary to speak in the plural." Jon could sit up. He could walk to the bathroom if not unescorted at least on his own feet.

"Tomorrow — "

"Seriously, Hank, why is that? Are you a committee? An automatic committee, whenever even one person is gathered together to practice his medicine? Or is it attaching to the long tradition — the Egyptians did some brain surgery, didn't they?"

"You've lost an eye, Jon."

"Did you ever think, Henry — sit down, are you sitting down? sit down and talk — about birth? About how much pain there is? Not the mother — that's different, she knows what it is, what it's for; but did you ever think about the kid? What an experience it must be, your whole world contracting around you, and then the horror of light and air."

Henry picked up Jon's chart. He looked down the list of medications.

"It would hurt to breathe, Henry, wouldn't it?"

Nothing there he could see. "I guess. I guess it would."

"You aren't sitting down. You can stay awhile, can't you?" Henry came back and sat down. "So, tell me about not being married."

"Nothing to tell."

It was almost impossible to read Jon without his eyes to look at.

"Didn't you hear me?"

"I heard you. I'm just — Henry, do you love men? Not *agape, eros.* Love men *eros.*"

What was Jon asking him, was Jon asking him — ? But Jon was married. And Henry might not be married but that didn't mean he didn't like sex, with women. "What do you think of me, Jon?" he demanded, trying to keep his voice level.

"A lot," Jon said. "Whatever your sexual orientation. Why, what do you think of me?"

The world. Henry didn't say it. He didn't say anything.

"See," Jon said, shifting up a little higher in the bed, "which is what I can't do, right now, which is getting me in trouble with you, Hank. David told me you were queer for him, his exact words; and I didn't believe him, because he lied and because — Well, frankly, if I were you and I were going to be queer for someone, I'd be queer for me."

"Jesus, Jon," Henry protested.

"Which you aren't, are you?"

"No," Henry said.

"So, why aren't you married?" Jon asked. "Or, more important, in love. Unless you are?"

"I'm just not."

"Have you ever?"

Unlike Jon, who was always in love with at least one girl, sometimes more. "Once I guess I could have, but — "

"I remember," Jon said. "I thought so."

"How would you — "

"It was my wedding. Janine, her name was Janine, she's Laurie's cousin from the Midwest. You said you'd call her, Hank, and you never did."

Henry had nothing to say.

"I've got her number," Jon said.

Jon waited. Henry didn't say anything.

"So," Jon said at last, "what do you think I

ought to do with my life, now that I'm going to have one?"

"I have no idea, Jon."

"Are you going to practice in Boston?"

"What difference does that make?"

"How should I know? What difference it might make, at some future time, is in the lap of the gods. I'm only asking. Pop would like it if I worked in the restaurant, but he doesn't say so."

"It'll be months before you can do anything anyway. Why not give it some thought?"

"Because," Jon said, "because . . ."

Henry waited.

"Because of the wonderful things thought does?" Jon asked.

"You're seeing a psychiatrist, aren't you?" Henry asked.

"Not exactly, no."

"Be serious, Jon."

"Why?" Jon asked. "OK, all right. Yes, I am. The trouble is, nobody there knew how much of the language I knew. Never underestimate the power of a linguist, Henry. So the good doctor has to spend his time writing down military information while what he wants is to find out if I'm secretly crazy."

Henry didn't say anything.

"Tell him I'm not, will you?" Jon's tongue came out and wetted his lips. "Unless I am?"

Henry shook his head, then remembered. "No more than you ever were," he said, "as far as I can tell. Jon, listen, you're blind in your right eye. When I was going after that splinter, the one I told you — I severed the optic nerve."

"On purpose?"

There was no way to deny it. "Yes."

"I didn't know if you'd have the courage. You have the courage to be a surgeon, so I hoped . . . You had the courage to kill that cat. Remember the cat?"

"I remember. It was choice I didn't have, Jon."

"That's your side of it," Jon said. "And then," he said, "even once you've gotten the kid safely through birth, if you do that, you can't know what life will be like for her. In the case of Sofie, or him, in the case of — I've got a kid I haven't ever seen, do you know that, Hank?"

"Yes."

"Take Ma, for example, she got out of Germany just in time and got her kids out, too. You'd think . . . but after fifteen years she has to be classified as an alcoholic, doesn't she? Doesn't medical science agree? Or Enid who will never have a child, thanks to the unmedical science of backstreet abortions, and who — she won't even consider adoption, Henry, and she's back home again, she says he walked out on her but — or Pop, who spent his life taking care of things for people, taking care of people, and there's always more being asked for."

"But, Jon," Henry leaned forward. "That was David."

"Or you," Jon said. "Is that David, too? Poor old David, all that responsibility, all that guilt. And nobody even knows who he was."

"What do you mean?" Henry stood up. "Do you mean he wasn't your cousin?"

"He maybe wasn't. Nobody knew, not for sure. I don't know if even David knew. Myself, I never thought he did."

"Wait. Wait, Jon."

Jon waited.

"If David wasn't David, he could have been anyone. He could have been — I can't believe your parents would have — if he wasn't — "

"But if he was, Henry. What if he was?"

"You just said he wasn't because you don't want him to be." By that time Henry was standing at the foot of the bed, his hands wrapped around the iron bar.

"Don't want him to be what, my cousin? Or do you mean Jewish? How much difference does Jewish make?"

"If he wasn't Jewish then it doesn't matter the same if he killed himself."

"When," Jon corrected him. "That. It's not," Jon said slowly, "who did what to whom that matters. What matters is that it was done at all. That it keeps being done. Stalin killed fifteen million," Jon said. "Just to mention one example. Fifteen million individual human beings. It isn't even only Hitler, Henry, and I'm tired," Jon said. "I'm really tired. I want to go to sleep."

"Jon," Henry protested, asked. Jon didn't answer.

It was afternoon before Henry had a chance to return. Jon lay quietly, his bandaged face staring sightlessly at the ceiling. Henry looked down at him. "Who's there?" Jon asked.

"Me. It's me."

"You sound terrible. We really never did know, Henry."

Henry pulled over a chair, and sat down. "Why tell me now?"

"Because it's time for you to settle the question of David."

"It's been settled for years."

"You didn't notice when we were talking yesterday," Jon said, "except for me. All of us except for me. You always used to notice things like that, Henry, the things that didn't match up. On the other hand, I'm no slouch and it took me a while to notice the exception, and that you apparently hadn't noticed it, which isn't at all like you, Henry. It's not terrifically credible, that's what I've decided. That doesn't seem too settled to me. Frankly."

"Why should I have to forget?" The harshness of his own voice in his ears surprised Henry, but it was time Jon got something straight.

"I don't want to forget — except that I wish I'd never met him, never — it's like this war, the least I can do is notice it, and remember it, not sweep it away under — " Henry couldn't

242

even finish the sentences. "I can't forget anyway. So don't tell me what should be in my memory, what to put into my mind and where — as if you knew."

"I wish I could *see*. I hope you're as angry as you sound."

"As if you always knew better." Henry stopped himself. Took a breath. "Jon, I'm so sorry about your eye."

"What's it mean, I'll see halves of things?"

"What you'll lose is depth perception."

"Really?" Jon smiled. "How are we to understand that?"

"As a fact," Henry answered, dogged.

"Wait, Henry — you keep bringing up the eye. Are you serious?"

"Of course I'm serious."

"Hank, you had to. None of the rest of it was your fault in any conceivable way; what was it you said? You limited the damage. Listen, Hank, I forgive you the eye, then, and now, and next Yom Kippur, and forever. I'm optimistic, I know, I'm a clown, but — if I'm correct, the word you carefully did not mention to me was hemorrhage. Which leads the inquiring mind to phrases like Brain Damaged — Human Vegetable — Better Off Dead."

Henry stared at him.

Jon added quietly, "Hank. We've served, and we've survived. We've survived David — I have, and I think you can — and we've survived this war — which is our war, whatever we may think of it. And I don't think much of it, truth be told. We should be drinking wine, out among the dancing women. The glass is half full."

"Maybe you're right." He had never been able to argue with Jon. He had never wanted to be able to, either.

"I keep telling you, I'm always right, even when I'm wrong. Maybe even especially when I'm wrong. What do you think, Hank?"

Henry smiled. "I think, there are a lot of times when I'd like to stuff a gag into your mouth, Jon."

The evening before Henry was due to fly out to Hawaii, then San Francisco, then Boston, he came by at dinnertime. Jon was sitting up. Only the bottom half of his face showed under the bandage, but his color was good and his half-face had flesh on it. The hospital table was drawn close to his chest and he was dropping chopped beef over his blue and white striped pajamas. All around him in the ward other men ate, either alone or assisted.

"I'll do that," Henry offered.

"Just because I'm hungry. Pride bendeth before hunger, it's an old proverb."

"Meat," Henry announced.

"You're going home tomorrow?"

"Yes."

"You'll have to fly and you'll probably get airsick." That seemed to give Jon satisfaction.

"Some things never change, Hank."

"And you're going to Tokyo the day after, and home in a week. Why did you reenlist, Jon?"

"I thought maybe I'd had it too easy. You knew that."

"Potatoes," Henry said. He had known it. "Are you satisfied now?"

"I think so. Yeah. God knows I ought to be. You know, you never told me what I should do with my life."

"I don't think anyone should give advice about something like that," Henry said. "How's your head?"

"I've felt worse. I've felt a lot better. But, Henry, you could just tell me what you think. You could give me advice and I could ignore it."

"Probably you should work with your father," Henry advised cooperatively.

"Agreed. Besides, my family's already settled into a house there. And Pop's getting old, there'll have to be someone to take care of my mother."

"Do you want to do that?"

"I don't not want to, which is near enough for me."

"On the other hand, that's not much of a life for you. Meat again."

"You mean it's not good enough?"

"Well it isn't, is it?"

"I'm a fine chef," Jon said. "Right near the middle of the second class."

"It would be a waste," Henry told him, "and I don't mean a waste of your degree. Unless you — Pears."

"Canned?"

"What do you think?"

"Then I don't want any."

"You have to."

Jon sighed, ate the bite, asked for meat and ate that. "How do I look now?"

"Better than you did."

"Because I don't want to give Laurie a cardiac arrest. Or the kids. Unless what, Henry?"

For a time, Henry couldn't figure out what Jon was asking. Then he could. "Unless you did something else, too, something you were good at, or had a talent for."

"Will you be in Boston?"

"You mean live in Grandy's house?"

"C'mon, Hank, you always liked that house. Besides, it's yours now. Besides, Boston's a good place for a doctor."

"Why do you want me there?"

"I told you once, you never did listen to me with proper respect — you're my best audience," Jon said.

Henry gave up, he did; he gave in, sitting motionless for unconditional surrender, his eyes on Jon who could not look back at him. On Jon, alive, and half blind. "Have some more pears," Henry said. "What about teaching? You've got degrees, and the restaurant's a seasonal business. You're probably a born teacher. Or, you could write a book."

Jon's mouth smiled. "A book? What, about this?" He spread an arm out to indicate the ward, and the country around. "Or about David?"

"Comparative linguistics?" Henry suggested; a mediocre idea, but he didn't care about that.

"Although I have a theory. You want to hear my theory?"

"No. This is the last of the meat." Henry sighed, audibly, smiling. "All right, go ahead, tell."

"I've been thinking about how wars historically have been used to synthesize a nation divided by internal unrest. It wasn't just the economy World War II healed, if you think about it. But that's not the way the country is reacting to this one, is it?"

"Maybe because it's not a real war?"

"It felt real enough to me," Jon said, bringing Henry up short. He'd almost forgotten — how could he have let himself forget? — what it was like to talk with Jon.

"That was stupid," he said.

"Or a good imitation," Jon agreed. "What I've been thinking is — I don't know what that means, or even what I think it might mean, but it might be worth thinking about. The Parable of the Barnyard Animals, maybe. What do you think?"

"I think that book's already been written."

"I could do it without pigs. The pigs aren't essential." Jon was grinning, so Henry popped the last of the pears into his mouth. "All right, the pigs are essential."

"If I'm around," Henry warned Jon, "I'll keep after you — "

"That's what I'm counting on. And in exchange . . ."

"Free dinners?"

"Free nothing," Jon said. "I've seen you eat. No, in return I'll dedicate this hypothetical book to you."

"I like that," Henry said. "To Henry Chapin Marr, without whom none of this would have been possible."

Jon laughed. "For Hank, who limited the damage."

Henry grinned, shook his head, leaned back in the chair, stretched, smiling. He'd go to Boston, live there, work there, close but not too close. "OK," he said.

"OK what?"

"It's what you've always told me, isn't it? Since I have to live my life, I might as well contrive to — " he searched for the word and couldn't find another — "live it."

"Did I say that?" Jon asked. "What a good thing for me to tell you. When did I say that, Hank? Did I mean it?"

Henry started the laughter, he couldn't help himself, and Jon joined in. Henry didn't stop himself, even though he thought it might well be inappropriate, not to mention incongruous, not to mention probably undignified in that place and time. Besides, he thought, as the sound of their laughter unrolled down the long room, maybe it wasn't.

About the Author

Cynthia Voigt is one of the preeminent authors for preteens and young adults. She has written eighteen novels including Newbery Medal winner *Dicey's Song*; Newbery Honor Book *A Solitary Blue*; and *The Callendar Papers*, winner of the Edgar Allan Poe Award.

Mrs. Voigt currently lives in Maine.